猜腦雷田

雅思口說

You don't have to be a one trick pony

7+

本書揭露4大低分真相，如何解決?!
由歐美影集敘述＋拓展思路＋影集語彙＋作者給力回答
➡ 不走冤枉路

詹宜婷 ◎ 著

MP3

低分真相1：回答內容毫無新意＋被考官認為不夠具體
收錄考官必問話題 ➡ 用最別出心裁的方式回應，PART2考試回答不單調

低分真相2：死背模板＋內容重覆性太高
特別設計拓展思路 ➡ 能舉一反三並活用背景知識跟語彙，擺脫模板路

低分真相3：回答生硬不自然
精選高分語彙 ➡ 活用高分語彙，於Part1+3考試與考官應答時，表達合宜又道地

低分真相4：無話可講＋答非所問
規劃影集敘述 ➡ 根植PART 2考試應考實力，考官提問時能充分回憶考點，不再與考官乾瞪眼

作者序

　　定居英國多年興趣為寫作及旅行。由於平時喜愛觀看歐美影集，希望藉由本書將一些道地的英語會話及慣用語呈現給大家，一方面藉**由五個主題劃分**【影集內容敘述】、【影集語彙】、【延伸話題】、【作者給力回答】及【話題拓展】幫助讀者們增進IELTS口說能力。另一方面揭露考生感到困惑之處，即**四大低分真相**，讓考生能少走冤枉路，本書也特別介紹許多英式節慶、習俗、知名景點等，希望讀者們能在學習英語之餘，也能藉由本書來了解英式文化。

詹宜婷

編者序

　　有感於許多考生對於在雅思口說應考，拿到成績後卻百思不解，在應答流利或與考官對談都很順暢，卻苦苦無法拿到理想成績，故規劃了此書，並揭露4大低分真相。

低分真相如下：

低分真相①：回答內容豪無新意+被考官認為不夠具體

低分真相②：死背模板+內容重覆性太高

低分真相③：回答生硬不自然

低分真相④：無話可講+答非所問

此外更藉由歐美影集敘述+拓展思路+影集語彙+作者給力回答五大部分協助考生獲取高分，進而少走冤枉路。

編輯部

CONTENTS

「暖身話題」

Friends ── Birthday Party

🌲 影集內容敘述

　　Monica 一行人正在籌劃著 Rachel 的生日派對，由於 Rachel 提到她的父母曾在她妹妹的畢業禮典上吵架，為了避免此情形再度發生，Monica 最後決定只邀請她的母親來參加派對。然而，在生日派對當天 Rachel 的爸爸不請自來。為了避免她的父母見面並發生爭吵，他們將派對一分為二，一半的賓客分配至男孩們的公寓，另一半的賓客分配至女孩們的公寓。Rachel 的爸爸待在男孩們的公寓，而媽媽待在女孩們的公寓。雙方人馬為了避免穿幫，不斷地在兩個公寓來回奔波、互相掩護，整個過程趣味橫生。

影集語彙

Look on the bright side

(釋) 原意為往光明的一面看，即在困境中正面思考的意思。

(例) Look on the bright side. Your insurance might cover the loss.

(中) 往好的一面看，你的保險或許能承擔損失。

Hit the road

(釋) 出發

(例) It is getting dark, we should hit the road.

(中) 天色漸黑，我們應準備出發了。

Stay clear of

(釋) 避免接近某人、某事、或某物。

(例) Please stay clear of dangerous animals.

(中) 請遠離危險動物。

Drop by

(釋) 順道拜訪

(例) Please drop by the office when you are in town.

(中) 當你進城時，請順道來拜訪我。

Dry out

(釋) 變乾

(例) Put the cap on, otherwise the pen will dry out.

(中) 把筆蓋蓋上，不然筆會失去水份變乾。

暖身話題

休閒話題

生活話題

常考話題

生活話題

 **延伸話題**

Bouncy castle

A bouncy castle is a large inflatable model, which can be used for birthdays, school fetes and festivals. Most parents hire bouncy castles for their children's birthdays, so children can climb, bounce and play on the bouncy castle.

彈力堡

彈力堡為一個充氣式的大型兒童遊樂設施，可被使用在生日派對、學校遊樂會、及節慶活動等。大部分的父母會在孩子的生日派對上，租借彈力堡供他們玩樂，孩子們可在彈力堡上攀爬、彈跳、及玩樂。

Birthday cake

Most British parents make personalised birthday cakes for their children. The birthday cake themes usually depend on their children's favourite cartoons or toys, such as cars, pirate ships, teddy bears or Barbie dolls. You can also put a personal message on the cake, such as "Happy birthday. Princess Anna".

生日蛋糕

大部分的英國父母會親自為孩子們烘焙個人化的生日蛋糕。蛋糕的主題通常會選擇孩子們所喜愛的卡通人物、或玩具等，如汽車、海盜船、泰迪熊、芭比娃娃等。蛋糕上也可以放置個人化的訊息，像是安娜小公主，生日快樂。

作者給力回答　MP3-01

- **copious** 豐富度　★★★★★★★★☆
- **creative** 創意度　★★★★★★☆☆☆
- **impressive** 深刻度　★★★★★★★☆☆
- **vivid** 生動程度　★★★★★★★★☆
- **pertinent** 切題度　★★★★★★☆☆☆

Wedding Party

The most memorable party I ever attended was a British wedding. The wedding was held in a picturesque town in the UK. I was invited to view the wedding ceremony in the afternoon. During the ceremony, the bride and groom made their marriage vows, exchanged rings and signed the wedding register. After the ceremony, guests filed out to throw flower petals over the newly-married couple for good luck. Guests can take pictures after the ceremony.

The wedding ceremony was

婚禮派對

我記憶中令我印象深刻的派對是一個英式婚禮。婚禮的地點是在一個風景優美的英國小鎮。我於下午時參加婚禮觀摩。結婚典禮的過程中，新郎與新娘互相宣誓、交換戒指、及註冊婚姻。結婚典禮結束後，賓客們在門口排成一列並向新人們灑花瓣，以示祝福。灑完花瓣後，賓客們與新人合照。

爾後進行的是迎賓

暖身話題

休閒話題

生活話題

常考話題

生活話題

followed by a drinks reception then a three course meal. During the drinks reception, I had a few drinks with family and friends in a beautiful British garden. All the guests have to choose their meals a few months before the wedding day. I had salmon salad for the starter, roast chicken for the main course and cherry cheesecake for the dessert. They were very delicious. The groom and his best man made speeches and the couple cut the wedding cake when we were eating dinner. After dinner, the bride and groom had their first dance. All the guests were welcome to dance after the first dance. After the dance, I said goodbye to the newly-wed couple and hoped that they could enjoy their honeymoon. It was a lovely day and I enjoyed the food, drinks and venue.

酒、及餐點。在迎賓酒宴上，我與家人朋友站在一個美麗的英式庭園裡享用美酒。所有的賓客必須於數月前先向新人告知所選擇的餐點。當晚我享用的前菜為鮭魚沙拉，主餐為英式烤雞，甜點為櫻桃起司蛋糕。餐點十分的可口。在用餐的過程中，新郎及伴郎特別致詞，而新人也在此時切結婚蛋糕。在晚餐後，新郎及新娘跳了第一支舞。賓客於第一支舞結束後進入舞池共舞。舞會結束後，我向新人告別並祝福他們有一個美好的蜜月假期。這是一個美好的一天，我也十分喜愛當天的餐點、音樂、及場地。

💬 話題拓展

★ **A British Wedding** 英式婚禮

★ **A picturesque UK town** 風景優美的英國小鎮

★ **A drinks reception** 酒宴

★ **A three course meal** 連著三道菜的餐點

★ **A beautiful British garden** 美麗的英式庭園

★ **Salmon salad** 鮭魚沙拉

★ **Roast chicken** 英式烤雞

★ **Cherry Cheese Cake** 櫻桃起司蛋糕

★ **Wedding Cake** 結婚蛋糕

★ **First dance** 第一隻舞

★ **Honeymoon** 蜜月假期

Notes

Lost ─ A Trip

🌲 影集內容敘述

　　三年前幸運逃離島嶼的Jack、Kate、Sun、Desmond 一行人在Ben的招喚下，一同前往位於教堂地下室的 Dharma Initiative據點。他們的共同目的是一同回到當年 飛機墜落的島嶼。該據點的管理者-Eloise Hawking解說 Dharma Initiative當初如何找到該島嶼、及如何再次回到 島嶼的方法。由於該島嶼不斷地在時空中移動，她必須預測 出下次時空之門開啟的時間點。她告知他們一行人須於三十 六個小時內搭乘Ajira Airways Flight 316返回該島嶼，這 是他們唯一返回島嶼的機會。Jack一行人隔天抵達機場並一 同搭乘從洛杉磯飛關島的航班。飛機起飛的數個小時後，如 預期地進入亂流狀態，在一陣陣天搖地動、及恐慌後，Jack 一行人順利抵達島嶼。

🚗 影集語彙

Leap of faith

釋 以信念去支持某些無形的、或未經證實的事物。指放膽一試，冒險去做某事之意。

例 I will take a leap of faith and believe them.

中 我會放膽一試的去相信他們。

Be my guest

釋 請便

例 當對方詢問你可否做某件事時（如拿走這份報紙），禮貌性的回覆對方可照他的意思去做。

例 May I take this magazine? Be my guest.

中 我可以拿走這本雜誌嗎？請便。

Condolences

釋 遇到有人過世時，向其家屬表示同情之慰問詞。

例 Mary heard the bad news and came to his house to offer her condolences.

中 Mary在聽到這個壞消息後，立即前往他家中弔唁。

Unpredictable

釋 無法預期的

例 Today's weather is so unpredictable.

中 今天的天氣真是難預測。

Sooner or later

釋 遲早

例 You should tell him, because he will find out the truth sooner or later.

中 你應該告訴他，因他遲早會發現事實的真相。

延伸話題

No-frills

No-frills businesses usually supply basic products and services at affordable prices. In order to keep costs low, some non-essential or extra features have been removed from the no-frills products and services. Common services include hotels, flight tickets, and supermarkets. No-frills products and services are very popular in Europe. As most no-frills airlines do not provide meals and in-flight entertainment systems, passengers have to pay extra to get these services.

沒有額外裝飾的服務

No-frills指價格低廉的基本產品及服務。為了要維持低價，一些不必要、或額外附加的商品特色皆被省略。No-frills產品及服務在歐洲市場非常盛行，常見的服務包括飯店、機票、及超級市場的商品等。大部分No-frills航空公司的機票不提供機上餐點、及娛樂服務。乘客需額外購買這些服務。

En-suite room

En-suite rooms are rooms with shower units. Most British hotels provide en-suite rooms, but some British hostels only provide basic rooms. Travellers have to share bathrooms with other guests. Most backpackers prefer to stay in hostels because it is a low cost option.

含衛浴的房間

En-suite room 即為含衛浴的房間。大部分的英國飯店皆提供含衛浴設施的房間，但一些英國的青年旅社僅提供基本房型。旅客需與他人共同使用衛浴設施。由於價格低廉，大部分的背包客偏好寄宿在青年旅社。

 作者給力回答　　MP3-02

- copious 豐富度　★★★★★★★★☆
- creative 創意度　★★★★★★☆☆☆
- impressive 深刻度　★★★★★★★★☆☆
- vivid 生動程度　★★★★★★★★☆
- pertinent 切題度　★★★★★★☆☆☆

Beamish Museum

I visited a well-known open-air museum in North England with my friend about three years ago. It was a long drive from London, so we stayed in Sheffield for a night and headed off to North England next day. It was one of the most interesting museums I have ever visited. It represents everyday life in rural North England in the early 20th century. It is a recreation of the history of North England and you could see the life of people who worked and lived here. The museum consists of a Victorian style town centre, a colliery village, a railway station and a farm. There were a tram, a wagon, and a bus transporting passengers to various parts of the museum. My favourite part of this museum is its town centre. It includes shops, a dentist's surgery, a solicitor's office, a bank, and a pub. You can see people wearing traditional dress walking on the street.

Beamish 博物館

三年前,我與朋友一同參觀了一座位在北英格蘭的戶外博物館。由於車程過長,我們規劃中途在Sheffield過夜,隔天再程前往Durham。它是我認為最值得拜訪的一座博物館。它還原北英格蘭二十世紀初的歷史建築、及英國平民的日常生活。此博物館包含維多利亞時期的模擬城鎮、煤礦村落、火車站、及農田。博物館內附有傳統電車、馬車、及巴士接送乘客到各景點。我最喜歡的區域為市中心。它包含了商店街、牙醫診所、律師辦事處、銀行、及英式酒館。人們皆穿著英式傳統服飾在街上行走。

The residential area is about fifteen minutes walk from the town centre. There were a church and a primary school next to the residential area. Coal mining was the major industry at that time and most of residents in this area work in the colliery. There was a farm house on the top of the hill. You can see farmers demonstrate traditional British farming machinery on their farms. It is a truly living museum. I felt like I was in the early 20th century.

住宅區離市中心約十五分鐘的路程，住宅區包含一座教堂、及小學。煤礦開採為當時主要的產業，而大部分的居民皆在煤礦場工作。在山丘上還有一座農家。你可以看見農民操作傳統英式農具。這是一座栩栩如生的博物館，我彷彿處在二十世紀初的英國。

話題拓展

★ **Open-air museum** 戶外博物館
★ **Colliery village** 煤礦村落
★ **A railway station** 火車站
★ **A farm** 農田
★ **Tram** 有軌電車
★ **Pub** 英式酒館
★ **Traditional dress** 傳統服飾

暖身話題

休閒話題

生活話題

常考話題

生活話題

Prison Break — Something You Want to Do

🌱 影集內容敘述

　　建築工程師Michael Scofield的哥哥- Lincoln Burrows 因被人陷害謀殺而判死刑。Lincoln 被關在Michael所設計監獄裡等待執行死刑。Michael為了營救他的哥哥而擬定一系列的劫獄計劃。他先將整座監獄的工程圖以刺青的方式刺在身上，再以搶劫銀行的方式入獄。經由獄中室友Sucre介紹下，他了解獄中的主要人物，及如何與他們合作一同劫獄。他成功地加入由John Abruzzi帶領的Prison Industries，及跟同在Prison Industries的哥哥見面，並跟他說明他入獄的動機。他也藉由進入醫務室及典獄長辦公室的機會，了解了監獄的結構，並規劃了一套精密的逃獄計劃。

影集語彙

Take a chance

釋 冒險

例 I don't know anything on this menu. I will take a chance and pick one.

中 我對個菜單的菜完全不熟，我會冒險的挑一個來試。

Grasp at straws

釋 臨危時抓緊任何機會

說 字面上的意思為抓緊稻草，意指在臨危時，想盡任何可脫離險境的辦法，即便是抓住一根稻草。

例 The doctor was grasping at straws when he suggested the experimental medicine.

中 醫生在臨危時抓緊救命稻草，建議用實驗性的藥物。

Have second thoughts

釋 改變主意

例 You are not having second thoughts about marrying me, are you?

中 你該不是改變主意不跟我結婚了？

Mull it over

釋 仔細考慮

例 He has been mulling over the idea of working abroad.

中 他一直在考慮是否要出國工作。

暖身話題

休閒話題

生活話題

常考話題

生活話題

Screw up

釋 弄糟；搞砸

例 He has been practicing it many times, he won't screw it up again.

中 他已經練習了好幾次，這次不會再搞砸了。

🎈 延伸話題

Warden

A warden is a person who is in charge of a prison. It is mainly used in the USA & Canada.

典獄長

Warden是指掌管監獄的典獄長。此字適用於美國及加拿大。

The prison infirmary

The prison infirmary is a room in a prison where prisoners who are injured or feeling ill go to for treatment.

監獄醫務室

The prison infirmary為當監獄囚犯受傷或生病時，所接受治療的房間。

作者給力回答　MP3-03

- copious 豐富度　★★★★★★★★★☆
- creative 創意度　★★★★★★☆☆☆
- impressive 深刻度　★★★★★★★★☆☆
- vivid 生動程度　★★★★★★★★★☆
- pertinent 切題度　★★★★★★☆☆☆

Anniversary Trip Plan

Last April was my wedding anniversary. I made a plan and gave my husband a surprise. My husband and I like boat trips, but we have never had a chance to go on one. I decided to find a perfect boat trip for our anniversary. I had done on-line research, read the previous visitors' reviews and found a nice boat trip. I chose the Broads in Norfolk. The Broads are a major network of rivers and lakes in Norfolk.

We arrived at the Broads around

結婚紀念日旅行計劃

去年四月為了我們的結婚紀念日，我計劃給我的先生一個驚喜。我的先生和我都喜歡乘船旅遊，但一直都沒有機會實行。我決定找一個合適的遊船之旅。我先在網路搜尋旅遊行程，並參考之前遊客的評論，最後選擇了The Broads, Norfolk的行程。The Broads為位在Norfolk一個主要河流與湖泊的通航網絡。

我們大約早上十點抵

暖身話題

休閒話題

生活話題

常考話題

生活話題

23

ten o'clock and it was a sunny day for sailing. We hired a small boat for a day and sailed it on the waterways. There were many things to do during the journey, such as birdwatching or angling. There were restaurants and pubs along the river. We moored our boat next to a restaurant and had lunch. We took a walk along the river after the lunch. The whole journey took around four hours. Its cost was reasonable. It was a fantastic experience and it is suitable for families. The whole journey was very quiet and relaxing and made me forget the busy life in London. I hope that I could go back to the Broads with my family or friends in the future. I would certainly recommend this place to my friends who are interested in boat trips.

達The Broads。當天的天氣十分的晴朗,非常適合遊船之旅。我們駕駛著租賃的小船在河道裡運行。在遊船的過程中還可以賞鳥、或垂釣。河道的沿岸有許多的餐廳、及英式酒館。約中午時,我們將船停靠岸,並在其中的一家餐廳享用午餐。午餐結束後,我們在附近的河岸步道散步。整個航程歷時四小時,價格也十分的合理。這是一個極佳的旅遊經驗,此行程非常適合家庭旅遊。寧靜及悠閒的環境令我忘卻了在倫敦生活的壓力。我希望將來有機會能和家人朋友們一起回到The Broads。

💬 話題拓展

★ **Wedding anniversary** 結婚紀念日
★ **The busy life in London** 忙碌的倫敦生活
★ **Boat trips** 遊船之旅
★ **On-line research** 網路搜尋
★ **Waterways** 航道
★ **Birdwatching** 賞鳥
★ **Angling** 垂釣

Notes

暖身話題

休閒話題

生活話題

常考話題

生活話題

Lost — An unforgettable experience

 影集內容敘述

　　本集回顧空難倖存者John Locke在飛機失事前的一些經歷。當飛機失事墜落在島嶼時，下半身癱瘓的John勉強掙脫輪椅，回想起到島嶼前的一些遭遇。John因與父親發生爭吵而墜樓，他雖然保住性命，却失去了雙腳。在他進行復健的過程中，Matthew Abaddon鼓勵他到澳洲參加短期叢林生活，來重新找回自我。然而當他抵達澳洲時，卻因下半身行動不便的狀態，被承辦拒絕參加此活動，他憤而告訴承辦：「不要跟我說我做不到。」他因回想到這些刺激，而在空難現場奇蹟似的站了起來，並逃離危險的空難現場。

影集語彙

Rain cats and dogs

釋 下傾盆大雨

說 過去的排水系統不佳，每當下傾盆大雨時，流浪動物的屍體會隨著洪水沖到街道。

例 It's raining cats and dogs outside, please remember to bring an umbrella when you go out.

中 外面正下著大雨，記得帶傘。

Stroll

釋 散步

例 I stroll along the beach with my dog.

中 我帶狗沿著海岸散步。

Supposed to

釋 應該

例 You are not supposed to drink here.

中 你不應該在這裡喝酒。

Call off

釋 取消

例 The football match was called off because of a storm.

中 足球比賽因暴風雨來臨而取消。

Skip out

(釋) 偷偷離開

(例) This customer skipped out without paying his bill.

(中) 這位客人未付帳就偷偷離開。

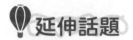 **延伸話題**

Walkabout

Walkabout is a way to experience traditional Australian aboriginal life, which involves travelling through the bush for a short period of time. It is a way to escape from the hectic city life and work.

短期叢林流浪生活

Walkabout為體驗澳洲原住民的短期叢林流浪生活。參加者通常藉由短期叢林流浪生活，來暫時遠離繁忙的都市生活，及工作。

Cross channel ferries

There are many ways travelling across Europe from the UK, by Euro Star, air or ferries. If you just want to chill out during the journey, travelling by ferry is an inexpensive and convenient option. It takes about ninety minutes from England to France. You can park your car on the ferry, go shopping on board, have something to eat and admire the ocean scenery. When the ferry arrives in France, you can just drive to the next destination.

穿越海峽的遊輪

　　從英國到歐洲有許多的旅行管道，像是搭乘歐洲之星、飛機、或是遊輪。假如你想要選擇輕鬆自在的旅行方式，搭乘渡輪是一個划算且方便的選擇。從英國搭遊輪到法國約九十分鐘。你可以將車停在遊輪上，在船上購物，用餐，以及欣賞海景。當遊輪抵達法國時，你可直接開車到下一個目的地。

 作者給力回答　　🔘 MP3-04

- **copious 豐富度**　★★★★★★★★★☆
- **creative 創意度**　★★★★★★☆☆☆
- **impressive 深刻度**　★★★★★★★★☆☆
- **vivid 生動程度**　★★★★★★★★★☆
- **pertinent 切題度**　★★★★★★☆☆☆

An unforgettable experience

　　My first part-time job in the UK was an unforgettable experience for me. When I was a university student in the UK, I found a part-time job with a catering agency. I worked as a catering assistant for a variety of places, such as weddings, meetings,

一個難忘的經驗

　　在英國一個難忘的經歷為學生時代的打工經驗。在英國留學期間，我曾在一個餐飲仲介公司擔任餐飲助理。工作外派的場合包含婚宴、會議、學校派對、賽馬場、足球

暖身話題

休閒話題

生活話題

常考話題

生活話題

school parties, a horse racing course, football stadium, and restaurants. Britain is a multicultural country with many immigrants of different backgrounds. This experience helped me to see multicultural Britain.

When I worked at an Indian wedding agency, I saw traditional Indian wedding customs, dresses, dances, and songs. When I worked at a restaurant in a football stadium, I saw many famous footballers. When I worked at a horse racing course, I learnt about British horse racing culture.

These were amazing experiences and something I hadn't seen in my life. Apart from watching British TV, the best way to understand British culture is to work with local people. I think I have made the most of my time in the UK. Since I only worked two to four hours per week, it was like a short break after a hardworking

場、及餐廳。由於英國是個擁有多種族、不同文化背景的國際大社會,這個工作經驗幫助我了解多重文化的英國。

當我為印度婚宴工作時,我了解傳統印度婚禮習俗、服飾、舞蹈、及歌曲。在足球場的餐廳工作時,見過許多的知名的足球明星。在賽馬場工作時,學習到英國的賽馬文化。

對我來說,這些都是前所未有且美好的經驗。除了看英國電視外,了解英國文化最佳的方式即是與當地人一同工作。我已盡我所能的融入英國社會。由於我每週只打工兩到四個小時,打工就像每週努力學習後的一個短暫

week. 　　　　　　　　　　　休息。

💬 話題拓展

★ **School parties** 學校派對
★ **Football stadium** 足球場
★ **Horse racing course** 賽馬場
★ **Restaurant** 餐廳
★ **Traditional Indian wedding customs** 傳統印度婚禮習俗
★ **Dresses** 服飾
★ **Dances** 舞蹈
★ **Songs** 歌曲
★ **Footballer** 足球運動員
★ **Schoolwork** 學校作業

Where the Heart Is — A person You Helped

影集內容敘述

　　位於Skelthwaite小鎮的兩名護士- Karen及Beth到一名獨居老人Wally家中做例行檢查時，意外地發現老人竟然獨自在照顧一名初生女嬰Tina。經了解，Tina的母親為他的孫女Katie。Katie為一名單親媽媽，因外出找尋孩子的父親，已經徹夜不歸好幾天了，獨留年邁的Wally在照顧小嬰兒。Katie也是在單親家庭下成長，她因與母親的關係不佳，被母親逐出戶，也顯少來往。然而，年邁的Wally已漸漸失憶，幾乎無法照顧自己，更無法照顧一名初生的嬰兒。護士們便前往Katie母親的家中尋求幫助。然而，Katie母親-Sarah對離家出走的女兒十分的反感，更拒絕任何的幫助。某日，Wally及小嬰兒突然失蹤，焦急的護士們再次拜訪了Sarah，並詢問Wally可能出沒的地點。一群人趕到了Wally常去的湖邊，發現他正把嬰兒放在小船上，準備乘船離去。在護士們的勸說下，他們一家三代重修舊好，並一同回到家中照顧Tina。

影集語彙

For someone (or something's) sake
釋 為了某人（或某事）
例 I prepared juice and coke for Cindy's sake because she can't drink.
中 我為Cindy準備果汁及可樂，因她不能喝酒。

In your dreams
釋 你在做夢
說 當聽到他人在講些不切實際，或不可能達成的事，你向對方表達你認為不可能會發生。
例 A: I think I can borrow £1,000 from Richard. B: In your dreams!
中 A: 我覺得Richard會借給我一千英鎊。B: 你在做夢！

In general
釋 通常，一般而言
例 In general, Japanese live longer.
中 一般而言，日本人較長壽。

Better off
釋 較明智的選擇
例 I think you'd be better off if you buy a house and don't try to rent it.
中 我認為你買房會比租房更好。

Make up (with someone)

釋 和好

例 Stephen and Nick had an argument yesterday, but they decided to make up today.

中 Stephen及Nick昨天吵架，但今天決定和好了。

 延伸話題

Social services

The goal of British social services is to protect children from getting injured. If there are concerns that a child who is susceptible to the potential harm, the children's services department will assign a social worker to work with the family.

社會服務

英國的社會服務目的在保護高風險家庭中的兒童受到傷害。假如孩子有潛在受傷害的可能性，兒童中心會指派社工人員協助該家庭。

Nanny

Nanny is a person who is employed to take care of children. Most working British parents usually send their children to nurseries, or hire nannies to look after their children while they are at work.

保姆

Nanny為照顧孩童的保姆。英國的在職父母通常將他們的孩子送到托兒所，或請保姆照顧他們的孩子。

 作者給力回答　🔘 MP3-05

- copious 豐富度　★★★★★★★★★☆
- creative 創意度　★★★★★★☆☆☆
- impressive 深刻度　★★★★★★★★☆
- vivid 生動程度　★★★★★★★★★☆
- pertinent 切題度　★★★★★★☆☆

A person you helped

I would like to talk about a person I helped when I was a student, I saw a disabled man selling chewing gum on the street on the way home. He had lost both his legs and just dragged and pushed his trolley on the street. I was shocked and didn't know how he could manage to drag a heavy trolley. I searched for money in my pocket and gave him all the notes I had. When I was about to walk away,

曾幫助過的人

當我還是學生時，我看到一個殘障人士在路上販賣口香糖。他失去了兩腳，僅用雙手支撐著在路面拖行，並推著手推車。當我看到這個情形時，我十分的驚訝，我不知道他如何做到。我找尋著口袋裡的零錢，並給他我口袋裡所有的幾張鈔票。當我正準備起身離去時，他將

he stopped me and tried to give me some chewing gum. I told him that I just wanted to help him and didn't want to have any chewing gum. He insisted on giving me some chewing gum. I realised that he tried to let me know he was not begging and this was what he does for a living. I felt guilty for not taking the chewing gum, so I took it. Maybe he had lost his legs, but he still kept his dignity.

After I saw this man on the street, I decided to help the disabled. I realised there are many people who are struggling with their lives in the world. If we could help them, it would make their lives much easier.

我攔下，並給我一些口香糖。我告訴他我只是想幫他，並不是想要拿他的口香糖。然而，他堅持給我口香糖。我才意會過來，他想讓我知道，他並不是在乞討，他是正當地靠賣口香糖在生活。我當時覺得非常的內疚，並未收下他的口香糖。也許他失去了雙腳，但他並沒有失去他的自尊心。

在目睹街上的這個人後，我決定幫助殘障人士。我了解到世界上許多人為了糊口而掙扎。如果我們能幫助他們會減輕他們的生活負擔。

話題拓展

★ **Chewing gum** 口香糖
★ **Trolley** 手推車
★ **Pocket** 口袋
★ **Dignity** 自尊
★ **The disabled** 殘疾人士

Notes

Emmerdale — Someone Who Helped You in the Past

🌲 影集內容敘述

　　因生活壓力過大而酗酒的Laurel，原本計劃與先生Marlon一同前往倫敦參加朋友的喜宴，但在聽說同一日舉行的Dan Spencer生日派對供應大量的酒品後，決定留在村莊裡飲酒作樂。她先和朋友串通好，欺騙了先生，找了個藉口留下來。然而，她在Dan Spencer的生日派對上，因飲酒過量而不慎失足從樓梯上摔了下來。她的父親前來接她回家，並照顧宿醉的女兒。當Laurel醒來後，原本想撒謊隱瞞酗酒的原因，但在父親窮追不捨的追問下，他才發現女兒酗酒的惡習。為了幫助女兒戒酒，他決定不幫她隱瞞，而將事情經過告訴女婿。當Marlon從倫敦回來得知此事時，十分的震驚，但他決定了解Laurel酗酒的原因，並一同陪她克服這個惡習。

影集語彙

Go off the rails

釋　表現異常

說　當一個人的行為漸漸開始異常，或做出與社會脫序的事情來時，可以用此句來形容他的行為。

例　He went off the rails recently and stopped talking to his family.

中　他最近表現十分異常，也不與他的家人說話了。

Twist someone's arm

釋　說服，或向某人施壓力，以迫使他做某件事。

說　扭轉他人的手臂，使他人覺得不舒服而妥協。

例　If you twist his arm, he might help you move the house.

中　假如你試著給他壓力，他或許會幫你搬家。

Speaking of which

釋　講到這個

說　當前段對話提及某事物時，通常藉由這個連接詞轉入這個話題。

例　Speaking of which, what is the status of this project?

中　講到這個，目前這個案子進展了如何?

Bear in mind

釋　記住

說　提醒他人之前所發生的事時，可用Bear in mind做句子的開

暖身話題

休閒話題

生活話題

常考話題

生活話題

頭。

例 Bear in mind that she is a vegetarian. Don't prepare meat for her.

中 記住，她是素食者，別準備肉品給她。

Chill out

釋 放鬆；冷靜

例 We went to a beach and chilled out all day long.

中 我們到海灘放鬆一整天。

延伸話題

Fete

A fete is a public function organised by a church or local residents. In general, a fete is held on a village green with many stands selling goods, homemade food and games.

遊樂會

Fete為教堂或當地居民籌備的慈善遊樂會。一般而言，在遊樂會上可見臨時性的攤位販售物品、居民自製的點心、及遊戲等。

Easter

Easter is an important festival for Christianity. It celebrates the resurrection from the dead of Jesus, three days after he was crucified. Traditionally, there are annual egg rolling competitions at Easter but in recent years they have been replaced by chocolate eggs in the UK.

復活節

　　復活節對基督教來說是個很重要的節日。它紀念耶穌被釘在十字架處死後的第三天死而復活。就英國的傳統而言，每年的復活節會舉辦復活節滾彩蛋比賽，但近幾年已用巧克力蛋取代。

 作者給力回答　MP3-06

- **copious** 豐富度　★★★★★★★★★☆
- **creative** 創意度　★★★★★★★☆☆☆
- **impressive** 深刻度　★★★★★★★★☆
- **vivid** 生動程度　★★★★★★★★☆
- **pertinent** 切題度　★★★★★★☆☆☆

Someone who has helped you in the past

Many people have helped me in my life. I would like to talk about one of my colleagues who helped me. When I joined my first company in the UK, I was very nervous and did not know what to expect. My

過去曾幫助過你的人

　　許多人在我生命中幫助過我。我想談論曾幫助過我之一的大學同學。當我加入在英國的第一間公司時，我十分地緊張，且不知所措。我的前任早在

predecessor had already left the company, so I had to figure out everything by myself. Luckily, one of my Italian colleagues in the same department was willing to tell me everything he knew about the company.

我任職前就離職了，我必須靠自己的努力來了解新工作。幸好，同部門的義大利籍同事很樂意告訴我他所知道的任何公事。

Since I had just joined the company, I had a lot of questions. He was very helpful and told me everything he knew, so I quickly got the hang of the job. I think it is difficult to find someone like him nowadays, because most people are busy with their work and they don't really have time to train new recruits. I learnt a lot from him and appreciate that he helped me.

由於我新加入公司，有許多在工作上不了解的事，他的幫助令我受益良多。現在的社會很難找到像他一樣的同事，因大部分的人都忙於手邊的公事，很難撥空指導新人。我從他的身上學到很多，也很感激他願意幫助我。

When I train new people, I remember his help and want to help new people in the same way. Even if I am very busy with my work, I still try my best to train new people.

當我訓練新人，我謹記他的幫助且想以同樣的方式幫助新人。即便我因工作而非常忙碌，我仍盡力地訓練新人。

話題拓展

★ **Colleagues** 同事
★ **Predecessor** 前任
★ **Get the hang of** 掌握做某事的方法
★ **New recruits** 新進人員

Notes

My Family — Something You Have to Give up

🍃 影集內容敘述

　　Susan在參加一次的抽獎活動中，獲得赴摩里西斯 (Mauritius) 的雙人來回機票。數日後，她收到由英國白金漢宮的來信，為答謝她多年來為慈善事業的付出，她將受邀出席位於白金漢宮的表揚頒獎典禮。由於這兩個活動的日期對沖，她必須放棄其中的一項活動。最後，她決定將免費機票讓與給孩子們-Janey、Michael、Alfie，以出席白金漢宮的頒獎典禮。由於免費機票的名額有限，Janey、Michael、Alfie決定用競賽的方式來將機票判給最後的勝利者。競賽的主題為放棄使用一個平時最喜愛的事物。在競賽期間支撐到最後，沒有使用最喜愛的物品者，即可獲得免費機票。有購物癖的Janey要放棄購物，喜愛音樂的Alfie要放棄彈吉他，而熱衷於電腦的Michael要放棄使用他的筆記型電腦。他們三人在比賽期間為了獲勝，彼此互設陷阱，趣味橫生。但三人最後都把持不住，在競賽期間使用最喜愛的物品，皆無緣獲得免費機票。

影集語彙

Wind someone up

> 釋　戲弄；逗弄
> 例　He is only winding you up. Don't take it too seriously.
> 中　他只是在逗弄你，別太過認真了。

Ring a bell

> 釋　聽起來耳熟
> 說　藉由提起某事，而勾起對方之前的一些回憶。
> 例　A: Does that postcard ring a bell? B: Yes, that rings a bell.
> 　　I remember it.
> 中　A: 這張明信片是否能勾起一些回憶? B: 是的，我想起來了。

Stand for

> 釋　代表
> 例　What does MBA stand for?
> 中　MBA是代表什麼？

In reality

> 釋　實際上
> 說　強調一件與實際情形相反的事時，可用in reality做連接詞。
> 例　Luke thought Ivy would marry him but in reality she is in
> 　　love with someone else.
> 中　Luke以為Ivy會跟他結婚，但事實上她愛上別人了。

暖身話題

休閒話題

生活話題

常考話題

生活話題

Worthwhile

釋 值得做的

例 This is a worthwhile investment

中 這是一個值得的投資選擇。

 延伸話題

Mauritius

Mauritius is a popular tourism destination in the Indian Ocean, which is about 2,000 kilometres off the South-East coast of Africa. Mauritius is both an English-speaking and French-speaking nation. Its main economy is based on tourism and it is one of the world's top holiday destinations with picturesque beaches and well-designed hotels.

模里西斯

模里西斯是一個位於印度洋的熱門觀光景點。它距離非洲東南岸約兩千公里。模里西斯為英語及法語普及的雙語國家。它主要的經濟來源為觀光業，並且也是世界上知名的海灘飯店渡假聖地。

Computer Geek

A computer geek is a person obsessed with computers but lacks for social skills.

電腦鬼才

Computer geek為形容沉迷於電腦卻不擅交際的人。

 作者給力回答　🅼MP3-07

- **copious** 豐富度　★★★★★★★★★☆
- **creative** 創意度　★★★★★★☆☆☆
- **impressive** 深刻度　★★★★★★★★☆
- **vivid** 生動程度　★★★★★★★★☆
- **pertinent** 切題度　★★★★★★☆☆☆

Something you have to give up

Something I have to give up is sweets and cakes. When I was a teenager, I was a bit chubby. I cared about my appearance at that time, so I decided to lose weight. I listed what I ate everyday and pointed out those fattening foods. I read some books about healthy diets and decided to avoid sweet stuff, such as cakes, sweets and sugary drinks. These are my favourite foods and I found it was

你需要戒的東西

我需要戒的東西是停止吃甜食。青少年時期的我有些圓潤。我當時十分重視我的外表，所以下定決心要減重。我將我每日的飲食內容列出，並選出那些易發胖的食物。我閱讀一些健康減重的書籍，並決定要避免吃一些甜食，像是蛋糕、糖果、及含糖飲料。由於這些都是

暖身話題　休閒話題　生活話題　常考話題　生活話題

very difficult to give them up in the beginning. I tried not to think about food at that time and concentrated on eating healthily and exercising.

After a few weeks, my diet plan worked and I lost weight. I realised that it was a good way to lose weight because I could still eat healthily but avoid high carb food. However, when I started to have a normal meals, I regained weight. After that experience, I realised that having a healthy diet is not just for a short period of time, you have to persevere for a long time. So I weigh myself and exercise regularly. When I find out I have to put on weight, I try not to eat fattening and sugary food. This helps me to keep a normal weight.

我平時喜愛吃的食物，一開始要戒甜食困難重重。我試著不去想飲食的問題，並專注在健康飲食及運動上。

幾週後，我的減重計劃成功了。我發覺這是一個很好的減重方法，因為我還是可以吃的健康，只是要避免一些高碳水化合物的食品。然而，當我開始恢復平常飲食時，我又復胖了。那次經驗之後，我才了解健康飲食並不是只限於一段時間，而是要持之以恆。所以我秤重且定期地運動。當我發現體重增加時，我試著不吃肥胖和糖類食品。這幫助我維持正常體重。

💬 話題拓展

★ **Sweet stuff** 甜食
★ **Appearance** 外表
★ **Fattening foods** 易發胖的食物
★ **Sugary drinks** 含糖飲料
★ **Cakes** 蛋糕
★ **Sweets** 甜食
★ **Healthy diet** 健康飲食

Notes

Neighbours — Something Did not Go as Planned

🌿 影集內容敘述

　　Amber及Daniel倆人期待的婚禮終於來臨了。然而，在婚禮前夕，Amber 的摯友Imogen向她坦白，她一直暗戀著她的未婚夫。Imogen決定將這份愛意藏在心裡，並不會出席他們的婚禮。當Amber告知她的未婚夫Imogen因個人因素將不會參加他們的婚禮時，Daniel充滿疑惑地詢問Imogen不參加婚禮的原因。Imogen坦誠她一直喜歡他，但她認為Amber 及Daniel倆人註定在一起，而她無緣與他在一起。當Daniel得知Amber所喜愛的戒指被丟進水井裡，決定冒險前往水井取回戒指。Imogen為了阻止他也跟隨他去水井。然而，水井的階梯卻意外損壞，倆人因此困在水井裡。Amber因準新郎無故失蹤，以為他們倆人私奔，傷心欲絕地取消婚禮。

影集語彙

Destined

釋 註定

例 This couple are destined to be together.

中 這對情侶命中註定要在一起。

Fate

釋 命運

例 It was his fate to board that missing flight.

中 搭上那班失蹤班機是他的命運。

Ominous

釋 不詳的

例 This piece of news sounds ominous.

中 這個消息聽起來很不吉詳。

Sisterhood

釋 姊妹之情

例 It was sisterhood that made her work hard in order to give her sister a better life.

中 姊妹之情使她努力工作，以給她的妹妹更好的生活。

Coincidence

釋 巧合

例 It was a coincidence that their birthdays were on the same

暖身話題

休閒話題

生活話題

常考話題

生活話題

date.

 他們倆人的生日同一天，真是巧合。

 延伸話題

Wedding gifts

When you are invited to a wedding in the UK, you have to prepare a gift for the soon-to-be newlyweds. The most common gifts are cookware, dinnerware, ornaments and furniture. You can also tailor-make wedding gifts for the couple based on their preferences.

結婚禮物

當你受邀參加英國婚禮時，需準備一份禮物給準新人。一般而言，常見的禮物包括廚房用具、整套的餐具、裝飾品、及傢俱等。你也可依照新人的喜好為他們量身訂做禮品。

Best man

The best man is usually the groom's best friend. A best man's job in an English wedding is to organise the stag night, make a speech and take the ring to the groom and bride during the wedding ceremony.

伴郎

伴郎通常為新郎最好的朋友來擔任。在英國的婚禮中，伴郎的工作是籌備男方的告別單身漢派對、準備婚禮致詞、及在婚禮上遞交結

婚戒指給新人。

 作者給力回答　🄫 MP3-08

- **copious** 豐富度　★★★★★★★★★☆
- **creative** 創意度　★★★★★★☆☆☆
- **impressive** 深刻度　★★★★★★★★☆
- **vivid** 生動程度　★★★★★★★★☆
- **pertinent** 切題度　★★★★★★☆☆☆

Something did not go as planned

Few years ago I went to Singapore to visit my cousin who taught Chinese there for one year. I visited a booking website and tried to find a nice hotel next to a beach. I found a hotel with a large swimming pool within walking distance to a stunning beach. Owing to the fact that I looked for the hotel at the last moment, I immediately booked this hotel. When I arrived at the hotel, it

不如預期的事情

幾年前，我拜訪了在新加坡工作的堂妹。她當時在新加坡教書一年。我在一個訂房網站上看到了一間緊鄰海邊的旅館。它附有一個寬敞的游泳池，並且步行就可走到海灘。由於我在最後一刻才開始搜尋旅館，我當機立斷的訂了這一間。當我抵達旅館時，它並沒有像網站相

was not as convincing as the photo showcased on the website. It looked like beach huts. The room I stayed in did not smell nice. It smelled like the previous visitors had a barbecue inside the room. Since the room quality was not great, I went to the reception and asked if I could change rooms. Luckily, they had empty rooms and transferred me to a new room.

The only good thing was this place was very close to the beach and train station. I had a nice walk along the beach in the morning. I am sure that some people like this kind of resort when they have holidays at the seaside. However, this kind of hotel is not my cup of tea. I've learnt my lesson and will check other visitors' reviews before I book a hotel next time.

片一樣的有說服力。事實上，它看起來像渡假村的小木屋。我住的那間房還有股異味，聞起來像是之前房客在房間烤肉的味道。由於住房品質不佳，我詢問櫃台是否能幫我換房間。很幸運地，他們剛好有空房，就幫我換到一間新的房間。

這個渡假村的唯一好處是它離海灘跟車站很近。我每個早晨都會沿著海岸散步。我相信一定有人偏好這樣的住房型態，但這並不是我所喜好的類型。這次我學了一次經驗，下次訂房前一定會先看旅客的評價再做決定。

💬 話題拓展

★ **Booking website** 訂房網站
★ **Beach huts** 海灘小屋
★ **Barbecue** 烤肉
★ **Reception** 櫃台
★ **Beach** 海邊
★ **Train station** 火車站
★ **Seaside** 海邊

Notes

Gilmore Girls — A Family Member You Lived with

🌲 影集內容敘述

　　Rory決定從耶魯大學輟學，並搬進她的外祖父母家中。然而，她與外婆的相處並不順利。外婆Emily與Rory的母親Lorelai的關係並不好，年輕時的Lorelai因受不了Emily嚴格的家規而離家出走。因擔心年輕的外孫女Rory重蹈覆轍，Emily對Rory的管教十分嚴厲。某日Rory夜宿不歸，也未打電話回家報平安。外婆心急之下在大庭廣眾對她訓斥，並揚言將她禁足。同時，Rory再次遇見舊情人Jess，並在他的勸說下，心生回耶魯大學讀書的念頭。在種種因素下，Rory決定離開外祖父母的家，寄住在友人的家，並計劃回大學唸書。

🚗 影集語彙

At the drop of a hat

釋 毫不猶豫地；不遲疑地

例 If you need help, just call me. I can come at the drop of a hat.

中 假如你需要幫忙，就打電話給我。我會毫不猶豫地趕過來幫你。

Errands

釋 差事

例 She has sent her child to run some errands.

中 她請她的孩子幫她處理一些差事。

Ubiquity

釋 無所不在

例 The ubiquity of TV advertising.

中 電視廣告真是無所不在。

It's a long story

釋 說來話長

例 A: Why was he in the police station? B: It's a long story.

中 A: 他為什麼在警局裡？B: 這件事說來話長。

Mock

釋 嘲笑；模仿

例 She mocked him because he acted strangely.

中 她因他的舉止古怪而嘲笑他。

 **延伸話題**

Drop out

If a student drops out, he stops going to classes before he has finished his course. Since it is getting more expensive to go to universities nowadays, some students can't afford the high tuition fees and decide to drop out of the universities and get jobs.

輟學

如果一個學生輟學，指他在未完成學業前，就中途停學。現今上大學的費用愈來愈高，許多學生負擔不起學費，因此選擇停學就業。

Sleepover

A sleepover means someone stays for a night at a friend's house. It usually indicates a party when children or young people sleep for one night at a friend's house.

在朋友家過夜的晚會

Sleepover指在朋友家過夜。它通常是指小孩或年輕人在派對或晚會後，留在朋友家過夜。

 作者給力回答　MP3-09

- copious 豐富度 ★★★★★★★★★☆
- creative 創意度 ★★★★★★☆☆☆
- impressive 深刻度 ★★★★★★★★☆☆
- vivid 生動程度 ★★★★★★★★★☆
- pertinent 切題度 ★★★★★★☆☆☆

A family member you lived with

I would like to talk about my younger brother. I lived with him until I was 25 years old. Although my personality is totally different from my brother and we have different hobbies, I still think I am very lucky to have him as my brother. We grew up together and shared our sadness and happiness. Whenever I am frustrated, he tries to encourage me. If I need any help, he is always willing to help me. When he got bullied at school, I also helped him out. I heard a lot of sad stories about

與你住在一起的家庭成員

我與我的弟弟在同一個屋簷下，共同生活了二十五年。雖然我們的個性截然不同，且各自擁有不同的興趣，我始終認為我很幸運能擁有這個弟弟。我們共同成長，共同分享喜怒哀樂。當我失意時，他鼓勵我。當我需要幫助時，他總是樂意伸出援手。當他受欺負時，我也挺身而出。我聽說許多兄妹、或姊弟因小事而產生紛爭，或互相誤會，最後

暖身話題

休閒話題

生活話題

常考話題

生活話題

59

unhappy brothers and sisters. They argue with each other for some small issues or have misunderstandings. They don't really talk to each other after arguments. Although we argue with each other occasionally, we make it up with each other quickly. It does not really affect our relationship. My brother and I live in different continents now, but we still try to make time and talk to each other every week. A good family relationship is difficult to maintain, I hope we can keep a good family relationship.

導致互不往來。雖然我們有時會吵架，但總是很快就合好。吵架並不會影響到我們姊弟的情誼。我目前與我的弟弟分居兩地，我們還是至少每週通話一次。

💬 話題拓展

★ **Personality** 個性
★ **Hobby** 興趣
★ **Sadness** 悲傷
★ **Happiness** 快樂
★ **Misunderstanding** 誤會
★ **Argument** 爭吵
★ **Relationship** 關係

Notes

暖身話題

休閒話題

生活話題

常考話題

生活話題

Gilmore Girls — A Special Gift

🌿 影集內容敘述

　　許久未見的舊情人Jess突然造訪Rory，倆人開心的聊起近年來所發生的事。Rory告知他目前從耶魯大學休學，並暫時與外祖父母同住。Jess則是在一次偶然的機會下，發表了他的作品，並受到一間出版社的賞識，出版了他的第一本小說。雖然初次出版的數量不多，他很珍惜這次的寫作經驗。Rory為Jess近幾年來的發展感到開心，同時也感慨自己漫無目的的過活，甚至從名校輟學。Jess將他的第一本小說送給了Rory，並鼓勵她再次返回校園求學。

🚗 影集語彙

Gist

釋 要點

例 A: Do you understand what I said? B: Yes, I think I've got the gist.

中 A: 你了解我要表達的嗎？B: 是的，我想我已了解要點。

Function

釋 儀式；社交宴會

例 I enjoy attending social functions to meet new friends.

中 我喜歡參加社交宴會，結交新朋友。

Prerogative

釋 特權

例 Driving posh cars is not the prerogative of the rich anymore.

中 開名車已不是有錢人的特權了。

Inspirations

釋 靈感

例 I need inspiration to create more new artworks.

中 我需要更多靈感來創造新的作品來。

Prudent

釋 謹慎的

例 She is very prudent to manage her family's finances.

中 她非常謹慎的管理家庭的財務。

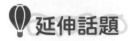 延伸話題

Gift-giving

Britain has a gift-giving culture. You receive gifts during some special festivals, such as Christmas, Easter, Valentine's Day and so on. If you move home, have babies, find a new job or leave your company, you also receive gifts from your family, friends and colleagues. All the gifts usually come with cards. The gifts do not have to be expensive, but they should be thoughtful and relevant to the recipients' interests.

送禮

英國是一個擁有送禮文化的國家。你在一些特殊節日時會收到禮物，像是聖誕節、復活節、情人節等。假如你搬家、生產、找到工作、或是離職，你也會收到來自於家人、朋友、及同事的祝福禮物。所有的禮物皆伴隨著卡片。送禮並不一定要送貴重的禮品，但能為收禮人設想周到，送他們喜愛的東西。

Staff Recommendations

Staff recommendations are lists of books recommended by bookstore employees. If you have run out of books by your favourite author, it is a good idea to have a look at staff recommendation books. It is interesting to know what other books book lovers are reading.

員工推薦好書

員工推薦好書是由書店員工閱讀後推薦的書籍。假如你已經看完了你喜愛作者的所有書籍，員工推薦好書則是一個不錯的主意。藉此，你也可了解其他愛書人目前在閱讀哪些書籍。

 作者給力回答　　MP3-10

- copious 豐富度　★★★★★★★★★☆
- creative 創意度　★★★★★★★☆☆☆
- impressive 深刻度　★★★★★★★★☆☆
- vivid 生動程度　★★★★★★★★★☆
- pertinent 切題度　★★★★★★★☆☆☆

暖身話題

休閒話題

生活話題

常考話題

生活話題

A special gift

A special gift I received was a history book about the kings and queens of England. I was very curious about the British royal family before I studied in the UK. Britain is one of the few constitutional monarchies in the world, but where did these royal family members come from in the first place? This was the question I wanted to know before I came to the UK. This book helped me understand the origin of the British history, a list of kings and queens and their stories. One of the most famous kings was Henry the Eighth, who married six times. Unfortunately, most of his wives were either divorced or beheaded. One of the most powerful queens was Queen Victoria, who had helped Britain to conquer so many countries in the world. The Victorian era was also a great expansion of the British Empire. The reason I like this gift the most is because it helped me

一份特別的禮物

我收到一份很特別的禮物是一本介紹英國國王與皇后的歷史書籍。在我到英國留學前，我對於英國的皇室十分好奇。英國是世界上少數君主立憲制的國家之一，但這些皇室家族又從何而來呢？這些都是我到英國前的疑問。這本書幫助我去了解英國的國家起源、歷史上在位的國王與皇后，以及他們的生平。其中一位最知名的國王為享利八世，他一生中結過六次婚。然而，他大部分妻子的下場不是離婚，就是被斬首。另一位最具影響力的女王為維多利亞，她幫助英國征服世界上許多國家。維多利亞時代也是大英帝國開拓疆土的強盛時期。我喜歡這個禮物的原因是它幫我了解一個國家的歷史背

to know the background of the UK and what people think about the future of the country. I think a good gift does not have to be expensive, but it should be thoughtful and tailored to recipients. This gift is a good example.

景、及人民如何看待這個國家的未來。好的禮物不需要昂貴，但應該是體貼且為接受者量身定做的。這個禮物就是個好例子。

💬 話題拓展

★ **Gift** 禮物
★ **Royal family** 皇室
★ **Constitutional monarchy** 君主立憲政體
★ **The Victorian era** 維多利亞時代
★ **British Empire** 大英帝國
★ **Henry the Eighth** 享利八世
★ **Background** 背景
★ **The future of the country** 國家的未來

暖身話題

休閒話題

生活話題

常考話題

生活話題

「休閒話題」

The Big Bang Theory — Halloween Party

🌲 影集內容敘述

　　本集敘述四個爆笑且缺乏社交能力的物理學家及工程師 Leonard、Howard、及Raj、Sheldon參加了由Penny舉辦的萬聖節變裝派對，所引發的一連串的趣事。四人分別裝扮成哈比人 (Hobbit)、羅賓漢 (Robin Hood)、索爾 (Thor)、及多普勒效應 (Doppler effect)。其中裝扮成及多普勒效應 (Doppler Effect) 的Sheldon，因裝扮的角色過於稀奇古怪，沒有一個人可猜的出來，大部份的人皆以為他是假扮斑馬。暗戀Penny的Leonard想要藉由這種社交場合與的Penny朋友打成一片，卻因自己的言論惹火了她的前男友，差點上演全武行，整個過程趣味橫生。

影集語彙

Fancy-dress costume

釋 化裝派對所著的服裝

例 David was dressed in Halloween costumes.

中 David穿著萬聖節的服裝。

Heads-up

釋 注意（提醒某事將發生）

例 I just want to give you a heads-up that the CEO will be in the office next month.

中 我只想提醒你下個月首席執行長將來到公司。

Peer Group

釋 同儕團體

例 These students scored higher on math exams than others in their peer group.

中 這些學生在數學測驗中所得的分數高於同齡群體中的其他學生。

Parades

釋 遊行

例 The parade will set off from the city centre at eleven o'clock in the morning.

中 遊行將會在早上十一點鐘從市中心出發。

暖身話題

休閒話題

生活話題

常考話題

生活話題

Anime

釋 動漫

例 Japanese anime has become very popular in the world.

中 日本動漫在世界上愈來愈受歡迎。

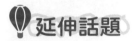 **延伸話題**

The costume themes

There are a variety of themes for fancy dress parties. For an occupation theme, you could dress up as policemen, fire fighters, doctors and so on. For an ancient theme, you could set ancient Rome, ancient Greece or ancient Egypt themes. For a fairytale theme, you could have Snow White and seven dwarfs or Cinderella. Other interesting themes include cowboys, medieval, Victorian era, science fiction, anime, fantasy and so on.

變裝派對主題

變裝派對有各式各樣的主題可選擇。如職業變裝派對主題，你可以裝扮成警察、消防隊員、醫生等。若是古世紀的主題，你可以設定為古羅馬、古希臘、或古埃及派對主題。若是童話故事主題，你可以選擇白雪公主及七矮人，或者是灰姑娘。其他有趣的主題包括西部牛仔、中古世紀、維多利亞時代、科幻、幻想等。

Halloween

　　Halloween is an important festival children look forward to every year. The typical activities you do for Halloween are making a jack-o'-lanterns, trick-or-treating, attending costumed Halloween parties, telling scary stories and so on. The themes for Halloween decorations are pumpkins, vampires, witches, ghosts and monsters.

萬聖節

　　萬聖節是孩子們每年最期待的一個節日。典型的萬聖節活動包含製作傑克南瓜燈、不給糖就搗蛋活動、參加萬聖節變裝派對、以及講恐怖故事等等。萬聖節佈置的主題像是南瓜、吸血鬼、女巫、鬼魂、及怪物。

 作者給力回答　　MP3-11

- copious 豐富度　★★★★★★★★★☆
- creative 創意度　★★★★★★☆☆☆
- impressive 深刻度　★★★★★★★★☆☆
- vivid 生動程度　★★★★★★★★★☆
- pertinent 切題度　★★★★★★★☆☆☆

A fancy dress party

I helped to organise my friend's birthday fancy dress party a few months ago. We had many great ideas about fancy dress themes, such as fairytale, medieval times, science fiction, around the world and celebrity fancy dress themes. Finally, we chose an around the world fancy dress theme because most of our friends come from all around the world. I decided to dress as Cleopatra because she is easy to dress up as. I went to a local fancy dress shop and bought a Cleopatra headdress. Since I have black hair and eyes, it suited me very well. My friends dressed as an Arabian king, an Aussie girl, a geisha and Bruce Lee.

It was fun because the first thing you did at the party was to guess who people were and where these costumes came from. Since the theme

化裝舞會

幾個月前，我幫我的朋友籌辦一場生日化裝舞會。當時我們有許多的化裝舞會的主意，像是童話故事、中世紀、科幻、環遊世界、名人主題等。最後，我們選擇了環遊世界主題，因為大部分的朋友們皆來自世界各地。我決定裝扮成古埃及豔后，因她是一個十分好裝扮的人物。我到附近的一間變裝服飾店購買埃及豔后的頭飾。由於我的髮色及眼睛也是黑色，這個造型與我非常地搭配。我的朋友們分為裝扮為阿拉伯國王、澳洲女孩、日本藝妓、及李小龍。

好笑的是，當每人見到對方的第一件事，即是猜對方在扮誰？這些變裝服飾從哪來的？由於化裝

was about traveling around the world, we also brought some authentic homemade food from around the world. The fancy dress party was successful and we plan to have another one with a different theme soon.

舞會的主題是環遊世界，我們也準備了一些道地的家鄉菜供大家品嚐。這個化裝舞會辦得十分的成功，我們計劃好再辦一次不同主題的化裝舞會。

話題拓展

★ **Fancy dress party** 化裝舞會
★ **Fairytale** 童話故事
★ **Science fiction** 科幻
★ **Cleopatra** 古埃及豔后
★ **An Arabian king** 阿拉伯國王
★ **An Aussie girl** 澳洲女孩
★ **A geisha** 日本藝妓
★ **Bruce Lee** 李小龍
★ **Headdress** 頭飾

主題 12

Melissa & Joey — Food & Cooking

🌱 影集內容敘述

Melissa的男友Travis到她的家拜訪，誤以為招待他的餐點為Melissa親手做的。Travis因喜歡這些餐點的口味，希望她能再次邀請他到家中用餐。事實上，Melissa完全不會作菜，這些餐點全是出自他的朋友Joey。在無法拒絕Travis的來訪，及無法坦誠事實的情況下，Melissa求助Joey教她作菜的方法。經過幾次的練習後，Melissa的廚藝進步，已準備好招待Travis。然而，當Travis造訪時，卻帶來她從沒有接觸過的海鮮食材。Melissa慌張地支開Travis並求助Joey。最後Melissa在無法掩飾的情況下，坦誠他之前吃過的餐點其實是出自於Joey之手。

影集語彙

Starving

釋 飢餓的

例 She donates £10 per month to a charity in order to help the world's starving children.

中 她每月捐款十英鎊到慈善機構，以幫助世界上飢餓的兒童。

Edible

釋 可食的

例 I don't think these wild vegetables are edible.

中 我不認為這些野生的蔬菜是可食用的。

Leftovers

釋 剩飯；隔夜菜

例 A: What are you having for lunch? B: Some leftovers from last night's meal.

中 A: 你午餐吃什麼？B: 昨晚剩下的飯菜。

Intriguing

釋 令人感興趣的

例 This is an intriguing travel book which contains many fascinating tourist attractions.

中 這是一本令人感興趣的旅遊書，其中有許多迷人的景點。

暖身話題

休閒話題

生活話題

常考話題

生活話題

Pathetic

釋 可憐的；可悲的

例 The student's work was pathetic. He obviously took no time to do it.

中 這位學生的作品真是可悲。他很明顯地沒花心思在上面。

 **延伸話題**

Mozzarella

Mozzarella is a type of semi-soft cheese, originally from South Italy. Traditionally, it is made of water-buffalo milk. Mozzarella is commonly used in pizza, pasta, paninis and salad.

義大利白乾酪

Mozzarella是一種半軟質的起司，原產地為義大利南端。傳統的製造是以水牛奶為主要原料。Mozzarella目前普遍用於製作比薩、義大利麵、帕尼尼、及生菜沙拉。

Ricotta

Ricotta is an Italian whey cheese. Its main ingredient is sheep milk whey. Since it is quite low in fat, it can be used as a substitute for other high fat cheeses. It is commonly used in many desserts, such as cheesecakes.

義大利乳清起司

Ricotta為一種義式乳清起司。主要的原料來自於羊奶乳清。由於它的脂肪占比很少，適合用於替代其他高脂肪的起司。它普遍用於製作甜點，像是起司蛋糕。

 作者給力回答　MP3-12

- **copious 豐富度**　★★★★★★★★★☆
- **creative 創意度**　★★★★★★★☆☆☆
- **impressive 深刻度**　★★★★★★★★☆☆
- **vivid 生動程度**　★★★★★★★★★☆
- **pertinent 切題度**　★★★★★★★☆☆☆

Cooking

Although I am not a great cook, I enjoy cooking. I learn cooking by watching cooking programmes and reading cook books. I like watching British cooking programmes to learn how to make European and international food. I learnt how to make gratin, French onion soup, cheesecake and tiramisu from these

做菜

雖然我不是一個好廚師，但我十分地喜愛做菜。我從料理節目及食譜上學習作菜。我很喜歡看英國的料理節目，來學習做歐洲及國際料理。我從這些料理節目學會做奶油烤菜、法式洋蔥湯、起司蛋糕、及提拉米蘇。英式

programmes. British cooking is very different from Chinese cooking. British cooking uses ovens to make pies, roast chicken, potatoes, and cakes. Chinese cooking mainly uses gas stoves to make stir-fry dishes. In addition, British meals are served in three courses- starter, main course, and dessert. I like the idea of a three course meal because you can expect something different for your next course. Chinese cooking doesn't have many choices for desserts. In fact, most Chinese eat more Western desserts than their traditional desserts nowadays. Compared with British cooking, Chinese cooking is easy to prepare. If I have a long day and just want to spend ten minutes in the kitchen, I would go for a Chinese meal. I also get inspiration by trying different foods at restaurants. When I eat some nice dishes at restaurants, I also try to make them at home. It gives me some ideas about what to cook at home.

料理與中式料理截然不同。英式料理主要是使用烤箱製作像派、烤雞、烤馬鈴薯、及蛋糕等食物。中式料理則使用瓦斯爐烹調居多。除此之外,英式料理的出菜僅為三道菜,即前菜、主餐、及甜點。其實我偏好英式的出菜方式,因為你可以期待下一道料理能來點不一樣的。另外,中餐的甜點選擇較少。事實上,目前西式甜點較中式甜點還來的盛行。與英式料理相比,中式料理較易烹調。假如你工作了一整天,只想花十分鐘在廚房做菜,中餐是個不錯的選擇。到外面的餐廳用餐也是一個找尋做菜靈感的方法。當我在外面的餐廳享用到一些美味的餐點,我通常在家裡試做。這可幫助我增加新的菜色。

話題拓展

★ **Tiramisu** 提拉米蘇
★ **Roast chicken** 烤雞
★ **Gas stove** 瓦斯爐
★ **Stir-fry dishes** 炒菜料理
★ **Dessert** 甜點
★ **British cooking** 英式料理
★ **Chinese cooking** 中式料理
★ **Inspiration** 靈感

Notes

暖身話題

休閒話題

生活話題

常考話題

生活話題

Gilmore Girls — Your ideal job

🍃 影集內容敘述

　　因受到舊情人的鼓勵，決定勇敢追求寫作的夢想。她前往當地的一間報社，並向編輯Stuart毛遂自薦，希望能取得一份實習的工作機會。Stuart一開始以公司沒有職缺的理由婉轉拒絕她，但Rory不願放棄，更積極地推薦自己。她故意將自己的作品集放在Stuart的辦公桌上，當Stuart發現時，斥責她不該闖入他的辦公室，並放私人物品在他的桌上。Rory受到斥責後難掩失望，但事實上Stuart已看過她的作品集，也願意給她五分鐘的時間面談。最後，她成功在此報社取得一份實習的工作。

🚗 影集語彙

On the spur of the moment

🈯 心血來潮的

🈺 We just booked the tickets on the spur of the moment and flew to Italy.

🀄 我們心血來潮的訂了機票，並飛到義大利。

Job opening

🈯 徵才

🈺 There is a job opening for a software engineer in my company.

🀄 我的公司目前在徵一名軟體工程師。

Qualification

🈯 資格；執照

🈺 What kind of qualifications do I need to become a pilot?

🀄 我需要什麼資格證明來成為一位飛行員？

Candidate

🈯 應徵者

🈺 Candidates applying for this job should hold a driving licence.

🀄 申請這份工作的應徵者需要持有駕照。

References

釋 推薦人；推薦函

例 My previous manager said he will give me a good reference.

中 我的前任主管說會給我一份很好的推薦函。

延伸話題

Organisational skills

A person with good organisation skills can manage his time effectively, work independently and take the initiative. Most positions require good organisation skills to achieve a specific goal.

組織能力

擁有良好組織能力的人能夠有效地管理時間、獨立工作、以及自動自發。大部分的職缺皆需要此能力來完成特定的目標。

Portfolio

A portfolio is a place to showcase a person's artworks and accomplishments, especially for a photographer or an artist. Most people build up a portfolio of work to show during their job interviews.

代表作品

　　Portfolio 即是展示過去成就及代表作的平台，特別針對從事藝術工作的攝影師及藝術家等。大部分的人在面試時，藉由Portfolio的作品集來展現自己的能力。

 作者給力回答　　MP3-13

■ copious 豐富度　★★★★★★★★★☆
■ creative 創意度　★★★★★★★☆☆☆
■ impressive 深刻度　★★★★★★★★☆☆
■ vivid 生動程度　★★★★★★★★★☆
■ pertinent 切題度　★★★★★★★☆☆☆

My ideal job

　　When I was a student, I always wanted to do marketing related work. I pursued a higher degree in International Marketing and eventually got a master's degree. It was quite difficult to get into this field of work because it is a dream job for a lot of people. Although I held an MSC in International Marketing, I didn't get my first job in

我理想的工作

　　當我還在讀書時，我就一直想從事行銷企劃方面的工作。我便求學並取得國際行銷碩士。由於行銷企劃是大多數人的夢想工作，這使得我一開始找這方面的工作並不順利。雖然我持有國際行銷的碩士，我一開始的工作並不是這行。當時的就業市場

marketing straight away. It was very competitive and most companies were looking for experienced marketers at that time. I worked as an account manager for my first job and moved to marketing after a couple of years.

In fact, my work experience in account management helped me to understand more about marketing. Sales Department and Marketing Department teams usually work closely, if I understood what sales people think about, it would help me do my job better. I was very lucky to get my dream job. I know most people pursue a job that is well-paid, but not the job they are interested in. You have to persevere to get what you want to do nowadays.

十分地競爭，且大部分的公司需要有工作經驗的行銷人才。所以我先從事幾年國外業務的工作，再轉換軌道到行銷企劃上。

事實上，我的業務工作經驗對於行銷企劃的工作有加分的作用。因業務與行銷部門總是密切的合作，假如我可以了解業務人員的想法，這使我在行銷企劃的工作上表現更傑出。我覺得自己十分地幸運能找到這份工作。據我所知，大部分的人皆追求高薪，但不感興趣的工作。你必須要堅持到底才能達到最初的目標。

💬 話題拓展

★ **Master's degree** 碩士學位
★ **International Marketing** 國際行銷
★ **Experienced marketers** 有工作經驗的行銷人才
★ **Account management** 業務工作經驗
★ **Work experience** 工作經驗
★ **Sales department** 業務部門
★ **Well-paid** 高薪的

Notes

暖身話題

休閒話題

生活話題

常考話題

生活話題

Baby Daddy — A toy in your childhood

🌿 影集內容敘述

　　Ben為一名居住在紐約的調酒師。某日回家後，意外地在門口發現一名女嬰。這名女嬰是他與前女友Emma所生的女兒，Ben決定獨自扶養女兒長大。某日，他發現Emma最喜歡的填充玩具Lamby不見了，他印象中上次看到Lamby是在大樓電梯裡，當時他正與一名剛搬進來的單親媽媽Kayla聊天。他立即拜訪她，並詢問她是否在電梯裡看到這個填充玩具，她否認看到。然而，Ben卻在離開她家時，看到與Lamby相似的填充玩具。他認定Kayla偷了Lamby。Ben決定藉由室友及大哥的幫忙，引開她的注意，潛入她家取回Lamby。但計劃並不順利，Kayla發現了並決定報警。在好友Riley的幫助下，Ben一行人登門道歉，但Ben卻不願把填充玩具交還給她，因他相信這是她女兒的玩具。然而，當天晚上，卻在自己家中發現兩個Lamby。事後，他對自己的行為感到非常抱歉。

影集語彙

Soon-to-be
釋 即將成為的
例 Jenny and Nick are soon-to-be newlyweds.
中 Jenny及Nick即將成為新婚夫婦。

Observant
釋 觀察仔細的
例 A: Did you just have a hair cut? B: Yes, you are so observant.
中 A: 你剛剛剪髮嗎？B: 對呀，你觀察很仔細。

Centre of attention
釋 令人矚目的焦點
例 The singer on the stage is always the centre of attention.
中 舞台上的明星總是令人矚目的焦點。

Miss the point
釋 未能理解重點
例 You missed the point of our conversation. Let me explain it again.
中 你未能理解我們對話的重點，讓我再解釋一遍。

Close the deal
釋 達成協議；成交

暖身話題
休閒話題
生活話題
常考話題
生活話題

> **例** After a long negotiation, we closed the deal.
> **中** 在漫長的交涉後,我們達成協議。

 **延伸話題**

Stuffed animals

A stuffed animal is a toy animal filled with soft materials. It is commonly used as a comfort object for children. The stuffed animal ideas are usually from cartoon characters, legendary creature or fairytale stories, such as Garfield, Odie, Teddy Bear, Peter Rabbit and so on.

填充玩具

Stuffed animal為一種塞滿毛填充物的玩具動物。它通常能給兒童一種安撫及慰藉感。填充玩具的靈感通常來自於一些卡通人物、傳奇故事人物、及童話故事,如加菲貓、歐弟、泰迪熊、及彼得兔等。

Toy blocks

Toy blocks are a set of bricks with various shapes, which children can build robots, cars, castles, villages and so on. In addition, toy blocks are also games with educational benefits, they can help children to become creative, learn different colours and shapes, as well as work with other children to build something together.

積木

　　積木為各式各樣形狀、顏色的小磚塊所組合成的，兒童可藉由積木組合機械人、汽車、城堡、村莊等。除此之外，積木也是一種益智的遊戲。它可以幫助兒童激發創造力、學習不同的顏色及形狀、及開發與其他兒童共同合作的團隊能力。

Housewarming

　　Housewarming is a party that people celebrate moving into a new home. This is an opportunity for house owners to show their new homes. Guests who attend the party usually bring gifts to furnish their new home.

喬遷慶祝

　　Housewarming為慶祝搬進新家的派對。屋主藉著這個機會來展示他們的新家。而賓客們也會贈送禮物給搬進新家的屋主。

 作者給力回答　🔘 MP3-14

- copious 豐富度　★★★★★★★★★☆
- creative 創意度　★★★★★★☆☆☆
- impressive 深刻度　★★★★★★★★☆
- vivid 生動程度　★★★★★★★★★☆
- pertinent 切題度　★★★★★★☆☆☆

暖身話題

休閒話題

生活話題

常考話題

生活話題

A toy in your childhood

I would like to talk about Monopoly. When I was a child, I used to play monopoly with my cousins. It was also my favourite game. Monopoly is an adventurous game, where you can develop your properties with houses and hotels, as well as receive rent from other opponents. Each opponent receives the same amount of money at the beginning of the game. They have to move around the board and compete with other opponents. There is only one winner at the end of game. The chance card is the most interesting part of the game because you can't expect what it is behind the cards. It is a matter of chance. This game is like experiencing an adult's life, but you don't have to take risks. It helps children to develop their maths ability because they have to sum up money and properties they own. In addition, it can help children to know about the

兒時的玩具

我小時候曾與我的堂弟妹一同玩大富翁。這也是我最喜歡的遊戲。大富翁是一個具冒險性質的遊戲，你可以開發房屋及飯店的地產市場，以及向其他的對手們收取房租。每個玩家在一開始皆拿到等質的金錢。他們必需在圖版遊戲上與其他對手競爭。遊戲結束時，只會有一個贏家勝出。機會卡是一個有趣的環節，因你無法去預測卡片的背面究竟是什麼，僅能靠運氣來決定。這個遊戲就像是經歷成人世界般，但你不需要去承擔風險。它也幫助兒童們激發算術能力，因他們須計算出自己所擁有的資產及金錢。我真的很喜歡這個遊戲，也認為非常有用。我未來也會與自己的小孩玩這個遊戲。

relationship between investment and risk. I really like this game and think it is very useful. I will play this game with my children in the future.

💬 話題拓展

★ **Monopoly** 大富翁
★ **Opponent** 對手
★ **Winner** 贏家
★ **The chance card** 機會卡
★ **Property** 資產
★ **Investment** 投資
★ **Risk** 風險

The Big Bang Theory — Wedding Invitation

🍃 影集內容敘述

　　Howard的婚禮在即，好友們紛紛確定會攜伴出席。單身的Raj也蠢蠢欲動，希望能在他的婚禮前找到另一伴跟他一起出席婚禮。他請遠在印度的父母幫忙安排一場相親。他與相親對象相談甚歡，但在最後一刻才發現她其實是女同性戀者。原來她誤以為Raj是男同性戀者，跟他相親的目的是希望藉由他做煙霧彈，以假結婚的方式，掩蓋她是女同性戀的事實。

🚗 影集語彙

Be dying to do something

釋 極想做；極渴望

例 Ben went missing. I'm dying to hear his news.

中 Ben失蹤了，我極想得知他的消息。

On the same page

釋 有共同的認知，理解

說 原意雙方共同讀同一頁，引申出擁有共同的認知及理解。

例 I need to make sure that everyone is on the same page to work on this project.

中 我必須確保每個人都有共同的認知來完成這個案子。

Compromise

釋 妥協，讓步，折衷方案

例 After a long meeting, two companies finally reached a compromise.

中 經過一個漫長的會議，兩間公司終於達成妥協。

Matchmaking

釋 作媒

例 Joan and Ken met though a matchmaking service.

中 Joan和Ken是經由作媒而結婚的。

Raid

釋 突襲

例 The police made a raid on a factory and arrested some illegal immigrants.

中 警察突襲工廠抓出非法勞工。

延伸話題

RSVP

RSVP derived from French "Répondez s'il vous plait" (please reply). RSVP is used at the end of invitation cards to request responses.

敬請賜複

RSVP起源於法語 "Répondez s'il vous plait" （儘快回覆）。RSVP 是置於邀請卡最下方，要求賓客儘快回覆。

Plus one

When you are invited to a social function, the person who invites you would ask if you want to bring anyone with you. You can use "Plus one" to let them know you will bring a person with you.

攜伴參加

當你受邀參加一些社交宴會時，對方會問你是否攜伴參加。你可以使用 "Plus one" 來表示你將與另一位賓客共同參加。

作者給力回答　MP3-15

- copious 豐富度　★★★★★★★★★☆
- creative 創意度　★★★★★★☆☆☆
- impressive 深刻度　★★★★★★★★☆☆
- vivid 生動程度　★★★★★★★★★☆
- pertinent 切題度　★★★★★★☆☆☆

A wedding invitation

I received a wedding invitation from one of my friends recently. They sent me the wedding invitation about three months before the wedding, so guests could book a hotel and plan a trip to the wedding. There was a RSVP card with the invitation card. I filled in the number of people attending the weeding and sent it back by post. The wedding was held in a picturesque village in Wales. Since the wedding was held on Saturday, I decided to stay in Wales for one night in order to enjoy a long weekend. I booked the same hotel as

婚禮邀請

我最近我收到一張朋友寄來的婚禮邀請函。他們大約在婚禮前的三個月寄出邀請函，以便賓客安排住宿，及規劃行程。隨著邀請函寄來的信中，附有一張RSVP卡。我回覆參加人數後，以郵寄的方式寄回給他。婚禮地點是在一個風景宜人的威爾斯村莊。由於婚禮是在週六舉辦，我決定留宿一晚，以便擁有多點時間，來享受悠閒的週末假期。我訂的飯店與婚禮舉行的飯店為

暖身話題

休閒話題

生活話題

常考話題

生活話題

the wedding venue, so I could walk back to the hotel after the wedding.

I set off for the wedding on Saturday morning and arrived in the afternoon. The wedding reception started at three o'clock and finished at eleven o'clock. I had a three course meal and a dance after the meal. Its food and venue were fantastic. After the dance, I said goodbye to the newlyweds and went back to my room in the hotel. After the breakfast next morning, I checked out and drove around the village. I left Wales around mid-day and arrived home in the afternoon. It was a hectic journey and I did not have much time to enjoy the scenery of Wales. However, it was very nice to see a happy couple again.

同一間。藉此,我可以在婚宴後直接步行回房間。

我於婚禮當週的週六早晨前往參加婚禮,於下午抵達飯店。整個婚宴為下午三點開始至晚上十一點結束。我享用了晚餐,並於餐後跳了支舞。餐點及場地的水準都極佳。在跳完一支舞後,我便向新人道別,並回到房間休息。翌日早晨,在享用完早餐後,我結帳離開飯店,並在村莊裡轉了幾圈。約到中午時分,我就離開威爾斯,下午回到家。整個旅程十分地匆忙,我都沒有時間好好的享受威爾斯的風景。然而,能再見到久未見面的新人非常地開心。

話題拓展

★ **A wedding invitation** 婚禮邀請函
★ **Guests** 賓客
★ **Plan a trip** 規劃行程
★ **Village** 村莊
★ **Saturday morning** 週六早晨
★ **Wedding venue** 婚禮地點
★ **A hectic journey** 匆忙的旅程
★ **Scenery** 風景

Notes

Gilmore Girls — A Weekend You Spent with Your Family

🌲 影集內容敘述

　　Logan的父親在美國麻薩諸塞州外海的馬薩葡萄園島有間渡假別墅。他邀請Rori、她的媽媽、及其男友一同到此島歡渡情人節。兩對情侶們分別悠閒地在海灘漫步、赴健身房運動、及享用情人節午餐。然而，隔天的早晨Logan的父親突然出現。Logan原本應於這個週末前往倫敦與其父親的同事開會，但他卻無故缺席。Logan的父親發現他在此渡假後，對他大發雷霆，要求他立即啟程前往倫敦。一行人只好收拾行李，敗興而歸。

🚗 影集語彙

Face the music
釋 接受批評或懲罰
例 He has to face the music after he was found guilty of fraud.
中 他被判決犯詐騙後，就必須接受應得的懲罰。

Nail in the coffin
釋 致命的打擊；導致失敗的事物
例 The evolution of the digital technology is another nail in the coffin of the traditional camera industry.
中 數位化的發展為導致傳統相機產業沒落的原因。

Behind the scenes
釋 在幕後地；不公開地
例 I guess that he is not the decision maker, there is someone who makes the final decisions behind the scenes.
中 我猜他不是最後的決策者，在幕後另有其人。

Back Burner
釋 次要地位；暫時擱置
例 Due to the lack of funds, this plan has been put on back burner temporarily.
中 因為資金不足，這個計劃暫時擱置了。

暖身話題

休閒話題

生活話題

常考話題

生活話題

Phony

釋 虛偽的；假冒的

例 He turned out to be a phony who had a fake qualification.

中 他最後被證明是持有假認證的冒牌貨。

 延伸話題

Martha's Vineyard

Martha's Vineyard is an island located south of Cape Cod in Massachusetts in the United Sates. The island is surrounded by beautiful beaches and walking trails. It is a popular summer resort for affluent families.

馬薩葡萄園島

Martha's Vineyard為位於美國外海的一個島嶼。整個島嶼由美麗的沙灘及步道環繞著，為美國富裕家庭的避暑勝地。

Burrito

A burrito is a type of Mexican wrap. Its fillings generally include meat, cheese and beans. Burritos are very popular in the United States and Mexico. It has been developed to a variety of choices.

墨西哥式捲餅

Burrito為一種墨西哥式捲餅。它的餡料包含肉、乳酪、豆泥等。Burrito在墨西哥及美國十分的盛行，並改良成各式各樣的口味。

作者給力回答　　MP3-16

- copious 豐富度 ★★★★★★★★★☆
- creative 創意度 ★★★★★★☆☆☆
- impressive 深刻度 ★★★★★★★★☆☆
- vivid 生動程度 ★★★★★★★★★☆
- pertinent 切題度 ★★★★★★☆☆☆

A weekend you spent with your family

An unforgettable weekend I spent with my family was a trip to Hong Kong. When I was ten years old, my parents took my brother and I to Hong Kong. It was the first time I went abroad with my family. Although Hong Kong and Taiwan are so close to each other, everything looked so different from Taiwan. I was only ten years old and was very curious about what I saw. I tried to understand the differences between Hong Kong and Taiwan, such as people in Hong Kong speak

與家人共度的週末

香港旅遊是我印象中難忘的家庭週末旅行經歷。當我十歲時，我的父母帶我和弟弟到香港旅行。這也是我第一次和家人出國旅遊。雖然香港和台灣距離很近，許多景物事物卻截然不同。我當時只是十歲的孩子，對一切事物充滿好奇。我試著比較香港和台灣的差異之處，像是香港人說廣東話，香港為右側駕車，香港有海底隧道等。我們繞

Cantonese, Hong Kong's cars drive on the left, Hong Kong's metro goes through an undersea tunnel, and so on. We travelled around the city centre, enjoyed the local cuisine and took the Peak Tram to the mountaintop overlooking Hong Kong.

In addition, my parents took us to children's paradise - Ocean Park Hong Kong. We rode on a roller coaster, travelled around the zoo and took a cable car to the summit. The view from the cable car was magnificent. You can see over the mountains and the South China Sea. However, my mum didn't enjoy the cable car because she had acrophobia. My favorite part of the theme park was the aquarium because I enjoyed seeing the undersea creatures. I was shocked when I saw sharks in the aquarium. I had never seen such a threatening animal before the aquarium trip. It was an amazing

了市中心一圈，享用了當地美食，及搭乘山頂纜車到山頂。

除此之外，我的父母還帶我們到兒童們的天堂-香港海洋公園。我們搭乘雲霄飛車、遊動物園，及搭乘登山纜車到山頂。從纜車望出去的景致十分地壯觀，可遠眺山景及南中國海。然而，我的母親有懼高症，並不喜歡搭乘纜車。我最喜歡的一部分為水族館，因為我愛看海底生物。當我看到鯊魚時，我十分地震驚，因我從未看過這麼具威脅性的動物。這是一次絕佳的家庭旅遊。由於我在香港擁有一次愉快的回憶，成年

family trip for me. Since I had a good time in Hong Kong, I still go back to Hong Kong now I am an adult.

後，我再次返回香港遊行。

💬 話題拓展

★ **An unforgettable weekend** 難忘的周末
★ **A trip to Hong Kong** 香港之旅
★ **Undersea tunnel** 海底隧道
★ **Peak Tram** 山頂纜車
★ **Mountaintop** 山頂
★ **Roller coaster** 雲霄飛車
★ **Acrophobia** 懼高症

Home and away — An occasion you were late for

🍃 影集內容敘述

　　大學生活充滿憧憬的sasha，為了準備隔天上台演講的報告而連夜趕工，然而，她卻因過度疲累而睡過頭，錯過早晨唯一到大學的巴士。sasha焦急之餘，趕緊打電話給學校教授詢問是否可延期上台報告。然而，教授要求她於當日五點前來學校繳交報告，否則本科將以未出席零分計算。由於下一班巴士為下午六點出發，她勢必錯過這個機會。正當她準備放棄之時，Matt表示願意開車送她到大學繳交報告。

🚗 影集語彙

Make a difference

釋 有影響

說 Make a difference指對某事、某人、或某情形有影響力。反之，指Make no difference對其無影響力。

例 The incentive payments make a difference to staff performance.

中 激勵獎金著實對員工的表現具有影響力。

Business as usual

釋 照常營業

說 Business as usual通常用於儘管在困難的情況中，依然照常營業。

例 Even after the recent plane crash, it is business as usual in all the routes.

中 即使最近發生了空難事故，航空公司還是照常運作所有路線。

One-off

釋 一次性的

例 This is a one-off concert. Don't miss out on this opportunity.

中 這是一次性的演唱會，別錯失機會了。

Take its toll

釋 付出代價

例 The falling dollar has taken its toll on the company's profits.

暖身話題

休閒話題

生活話題

常考話題

生活話題

中 公司的利潤因美元貶值而付出相當大的代價。

Hectic

釋 忙碌的

例 I had a hectic weekend because I was doing up my house.

中 我的週末十分忙碌，因為我需要整修我的房子。

 **延伸話題**

Presentation

A presentation is a verbal report with illustrative graphs a presenter delivers to a large audience. University students usually need to present their studies to their lecturers and classmates. It helps to enhance students' communication skills and improve the degree of self-confidence.

簡報

簡報為以口頭報告的方法向觀眾傳達訊息、或觀點。簡報過程中也會展示相關的圖示說明，以利理解口頭報告。大學學生通常需要向講師或同學報告他們的學習研究。這可幫助學生的表達能力，及加強自信度。

Assessment

In British universities, an assessment is a report written by an instructor regarding the evaluation of a student's achievement on a course.

評估

　　在英國的大學裡，評估為由講師所撰寫關於學生在課堂上學業表現的報告。

 作者給力回答　　MP3-17

- copious 豐富度　★★★★★★★★★☆
- creative 創意度　★★★★★★★☆☆☆
- impressive 深刻度　★★★★★★★★☆☆
- vivid 生動程度　★★★★★★★★★☆
- pertinent 切題度　★★★★★★☆☆☆

An occasion I was late for

　　I would like to talk about a trip to China. When I visited one of my friends in Guangzhou a few years ago, I planned to take a ferry from Hong Kong to Guangzhou. It was my first time to take a ferry in Hong Kong. The departure time was seven o'clock in the evening. I thought I had to arrive fifteen minutes before

遲到事件

　　我想要談一次到中國旅行的經驗。幾年前，當我赴廣州拜訪一位朋友時，我計劃從香港搭乘渡輪到廣州。當時是我生平第一次在香港搭乘渡輪。渡輪的出發時間為晚上七點鐘。我原本以為只需在出發前的十五分鐘抵達即

暖身話題

休閒話題

生活話題

常考話題

生活話題

the departure time. When I arrived there, the gate had already closed five minutes before. I realised that I had to be at the gate around twenty minutes before the departure time. It was just like taking an airplane. I was shocked and didn't know what to do.

I called my friend immediately and explained the situation. She suggested that I take the next ferry to Zhongshan and she would pick me up from that port. I bought a ticket and took the next ferry to Zhongshan. I felt very sorry for my friend because she had to drive further to pick me up. I really appreciated her help, so I arrived there safe and sound. In order to say thank you to her, I went to her favourite shop and bought her a nice gift. Since then whenever I go traveling to places I am not familiar with, I arrive there early.

可。然而，當我抵達港口時，閘口已經在五分鐘前關閉了。我才了解搭乘渡輪就像搭飛機一樣，必須於出發前二十分鐘抵達閘口。

我當時很驚慌且不知所措。我立即打了通電話給我的朋友，並告知她我的狀況。她建議我可以搭乘下一班渡輪到中山，她可以在那個港口接我。我買了船票後，即搭乘下一班渡輪前往中山。我當時對我的朋友感到很抱歉，因為她必須多花一些路程來接我。我十分感謝她的幫忙，我才能平安地抵達。為了答謝她的幫助，我在她最喜歡的商店買了一個禮物送給她。從那之後每當我在旅行時，若到不熟悉的地方，我會提早抵達來了解實際的狀況。

話題拓展

★ **A trip to China** 中國之旅
★ **Ferry** 渡輪
★ **Departure time** 出發時間
★ **Gate** 閘門
★ **Port** 港口
★ **Favourite shop** 最喜歡的商店
★ **Safe and sound** 安然無恙

Notes

暖身話題

休閒話題

生活話題

常考話題

生活話題

Neighbours — A child

🌲 影集內容敘述

　　單身且事業有成的Lucy想要擁有自己的小孩，卻不想走進婚姻生活。她決定向朋友Chris借種，以人工受孕的方式懷孕。Chris不想單純的只做一位捐贈者，他想定期的探望孩子，陪伴他一起長大。試孕成功後，倆人開心地赴醫院做超音波檢查，及討論將來的寶寶房間的佈置等育兒問題。由於Lucy長期定居於紐約，考慮在紐約扶養孩子長大。她邀請Chris一起到紐約居住，共同扶養孩子長大。然而，對於離開澳洲，Chris除了事業，還有感情的因素需考量。為了孩子的未來，Chris當機立斷地決定與Lucy前往紐約開創新生活。

影集語彙

Stepping stone

釋　跳板

說　原意指在河流中的踏腳石，藉由踏腳石來渡過湍急的溪流。延伸為達成目標的一個跳板。

例　Linda hates her job but it is just a stepping stone for her to get a better job.

中　Linda厭惡她的工作，但這個工作只是幫她找到更好工作的一個跳板。

Keep an eye on

釋　仔細看守

例　Could you please keep an eye on my baby when I go to the toilet?

中　我去廁所時，可以幫我看守我的孩子嗎？

Crave

釋　渴望得到

例　When Sue was pregnant, she craved spicy food.

中　當Sue懷孕時，她常渴望吃辣食。

Jet lag

釋　時差

例　I have got bad jet lag and need to rest.

中　我深受時差之苦，需要休息一下。

暖身話題
休閒話題
生活話題
常考話題
生活話題

Fatherhood

釋 父親的身分

例 The joy of fatherhood has changed him into a caring man.

中 當爸爸的喜悅讓他改變為一位有愛心的人。

 延伸話題

Nursery

Nursery is a place where young children and babies are temporarily taken care of while their parents are working. Nursery is also a place where plants and trees are grown.

托兒所

當父母在工作時，Nursery為臨時托管兒童或嬰兒的場所。Nursery也指種植花草樹木的苗圃。

Morning sickness

Morning sickness is a feeling of nausea and vomiting during early pregnancy.

晨吐

Morning sickness為懷孕初期，孕婦感覺噁心及想吐的一種感覺。

作者給力回答　MP3-18

- **copious** 豐富度　★★★★★★★★★☆
- **creative** 創意度　★★★★★★☆☆☆
- **impressive** 深刻度　★★★★★★★★☆☆
- **vivid** 生動程度　★★★★★★★★★☆
- **pertinent** 切題度　★★★★★★☆☆☆

A Child

I want to talk about one of my friend's daughters. She was about seven years old when I first met her. She grew up in a large family with many older brothers, sisters, and cousins. Since she was the youngest child in the family, she was so spoiled by her grandparents, uncles, and aunts.

She likes playing games and cards with older siblings and cousins and pretends to speak like an adult when she talks to them. She is a confident, outgoing girl, as well as a

孩子

我想要談我一位朋友的女兒。當我第一次見她時，她大約七歲大。她成長於一個大家族，並擁有許多哥哥、姊姊、堂哥、及堂姊。由於她是家中最小的孩子，她十分的受寵。

她喜歡與其他年長的兄姊一起玩牌及遊戲，並學大人說話的方式與兄姊們溝通。她是一個有自信且外向的女孩，並且學習

暖身話題

休閒話題

生活話題

常考話題

生活話題

quick learner. If there is no logic in what you say, she even corrects you. I guess she takes after her parents because both her parents are very smart and have professional jobs. She is ten years old this year and is studying at a well-known primary school.

When I visited her last month, I brought some toys and clothes for her. After having a chat with her recently, I realised that she is growing very fast, and I am getting older. Sooner or later, she will go to university and have her own life. It is interesting to watch a child growing into a teenager, which reminds me of my childhood. It's like seeing someone who is taking a similar path as you. It makes me want to give her some advice based on my experience.

能力強。假如你説的話沒有邏輯，她甚至能糾正你。我猜她是像她的父母，因為她的父母皆十分聰明且擁有專業的工作。她今年剛滿十歲，在一間知名的小學讀書。

我上個月剛探望她，並買了一些玩具及衣服給她。在和她聊天後，我發覺她長大了，而我也老了。在過不久，她就會上大學，並開啟她的人生。看著她成長為青少年是一件有趣的事，也讓我回想起我的童年，就像看著一個人也走著自己曾走過的道路。這也讓我想藉由自身的經驗，給她一些人生上的建議。

💬 話題拓展

★ **Sibling** 兄弟姊妹
★ **Logic** 邏輯
★ **Cards** 紙牌遊戲
★ **Primary school** 英國的小學
★ **Advice** 忠告
★ **Toys** 玩具
★ **Clothes** 衣服

Notes

Neighbours — Animals

🍃 影集內容敘述

　　Ramsay Street發現了一條走失的拉不拉多犬，在為她找到主人之前，她先寄住在愛狗人士Lucy的家。然而，尋找狗主人的過程卻一直不順利。但在一次DNA的檢驗後，發現它是Lucy之前的愛犬—Bouncer 的後裔。Lucy驚喜之餘，也決定將Bouncer二代留在Robinson家族。Lucy因決定回紐約待產，將Bouncer二代寄託給在對抗病魔的哥哥Paul照顧，希望藉由Bouncer二代的陪伴，他的病情能好轉。

影集語彙

Fair enough

釋　有道理；說得對。

例　A: I don't think I should spend money on computer games because I am unemployed. B: Fair enough.

中　A: 由於我目前沒有工作，我覺得我不應該花錢在電玩遊戲上。B:說得有道理。

Descendant

釋　子孫；後代

例　She is a descendant of the royal family.

中　她是皇室家族的後代。

Hush-hush

釋　極祕密的

例　Keep Emma's surprise birthday party hush-hush. We don't want her to find out.

中　Emma的生日驚喜派對是極祕密的。我們不想讓她發現。

Track down

釋　追蹤到；追查到

例　He took one year to track this missing person down.

中　他花了一年的時間追蹤到這個失蹤人口。

暖身話題

休閒話題

生活話題

常考話題

生活話題

Turn out to be

釋 原來是；證明是

例 Looking after a baby turned out to be harder than I thought.

中 照顧小嬰兒比我想像中的還要難。

 延伸話題

Animal shelter

An animal shelter is a place where abandoned and stray animals get temporary housing. Some animal shelters also help to find new owners for these animals.

動物收容所

Animal shelter為收容遺棄及流浪動物的臨時收容所。一些動物收容所還會協助這些動物找到新的主人。

Breeder

A breeder is a person who breeds animals or plants. A breeder selects specimens of the same breed to reproduce the same kind of animals or plants.

飼養動物、培育植物的人

Breeder為飼養、繁殖動物的人、或培育植物的人。他們選擇相同品種的樣本來繁殖同類的動植物。

- copious 豐富度　★★★★★★★★★☆
- creative 創意度　★★★★★★☆☆☆
- impressive 深刻度　★★★★★★★★☆☆
- vivid 生動程度　★★★★★★★★★☆
- pertinent 切題度　★★★★★★★☆☆☆

An animal

When I was a child, my family had a Japanese Spitz. Since she had beautiful soft white fur, we called her Snowy. She was a tame and smart dog as well as a good listener. When I was sad and lonely, I came to talk to her and she made me feel better. She also protected me from getting hurt by other dogs. She was very observant. When she saw suspicious strangers, she barked at them. Since my father owned a business at that time, she helped to keep an eye out for burglars. She was a guard dog for my father's business. She was also

動物

當我還小時，我家收養了一隻狐狸狗。由於她擁有美麗柔順的白毛，我們叫她小白。她是一隻溫馴聰明的狗，而且也是一個傾聽者。當我難過孤單時，我會說給她聽，讓我覺得安慰。她也保護我，不讓其他的狗欺負我。她觀察靈敏，一旦見到形跡可疑的陌生人，就會對他們吠叫。我的父親當時經營生意，她也隨時注意夜賊。她也是我父親生意的看家犬。她也是我童年最

暖身話題

休閒話題

生活話題

常考話題

生活話題

my best friend and we had a lot of pleasant memories during my childhood.

Unfortunately, she died from an accident. My brother and I were very sad about this bad news and couldn't believe it. She had lived with us for around seven years before she passed away. She had many puppies when she was alive. One of her daughters looked exactly the same as her, so we called her Snowy II. We kept Snowy II in our family and we were glad she left her precious daughter to us. One of the important things I learnt from her was life is short. We should always enjoy our lives with our family and friends.

好的朋友，我們有許多愉快的回憶。

遺憾地，她後來因意外過世了。我和弟弟皆十分的難過，也不願相信事實。在她過世前，她與我們共同生活了七年之久。她生前也有許多小狗，其中的一隻小狗幾乎長得跟她一模一樣，我們叫她小白二世，並將她留在我們的家生活。我們很開心小白將她珍貴的女兒留給了我們。我從小白身上學到的一件事是，珍惜身邊的家人及朋友，因為時光很短暫。

💬 話題拓展

★ **Listener** 傾聽者
★ **Burglars** 夜賊
★ **Strangers** 陌生人
★ **Guard dog** 看家犬
★ **Puppies** 小狗
★ **Family** 家庭
★ **Friends** 朋友

Notes

主題
20

Rules of Engagement — A reunion

🌳 影集內容敘述

　　期待已久的高中同學會即將到來，Audrey心中所想的即是向在加拿大老家的同窗炫耀她在紐約多采多姿的生活。Audrey到紐約發展多年，擁有一個令人稱羨的工作，及一段幸福美滿的婚姻生活。然而，在她抵達同學會後，她發現她並不是同學中最成功的一位，大部分的同學皆事業成功，及家庭圓滿。在她失落之時，台上突然宣佈她獲得本次同學會抽 活動的頭獎。她興奮地上台領獎。但當她得知獎品是免費住宿一晚位於紐約中央公園南的公寓時，對於住在紐約的她，覺得有些諷刺。

影集語彙

Out of curiosity

釋 出於好奇

例 Just out of curiosity, why did you immigrate to New Zealand?

中 只是出於好奇，你為什麼移民紐西蘭？

Lame

釋 缺乏說服力的

例 Ben did not hand over his report on time and made a lame excuse to his instructor.

中 Ben沒有準時繳交報告，並向教授編了一個無說服力的藉口。

Old-fashioned

釋 過時的；老式的

例 Julia's grandmother keeps a lot of old-fashioned clothes.

中 Julia的奶奶保留著許多老式的衣服。

To the extent

釋 到…程度

例 His company has made a loss to the extent of one million dollars.

中 他的公司虧損的金額達到一百萬美元。

Impress

釋 給…留下深刻印象

例 I am impressed by his generosity.

中 我對他的慷慨大方留下深刻的印象。

延伸話題

Raffle

A raffle is a competition in which people buy tickets with different numbers. Each ticket will have chance to win a prize.

獎券

Raffle為玩家購買不同號碼獎券的抽獎活動。每張獎券都有機會贏得獎項。

Central Park

Central Park is a large urban park, which is located in the central part of Manhattan, New York City. It has many popular attractions, such as a man-made lake, ice-skating rink, zoo, carousel and so on. Central Park is an oasis in the city for both residents and tourists.

中央公園

中央公園為紐約曼哈頓市中心的一座大型公園。公園內設有許多熱門的景點，像是人工湖、溜冰場、動物園、及旋轉木馬等。對當地居民及觀光客而言，中央公園就像是在都會中的一座綠州，供人休憩及健身。

 作者給力回答　　MP3-20

- copious 豐富度　★★★★★★★★★☆
- creative 創意度　★★★★★★☆☆☆
- impressive 深刻度　★★★★★★★☆☆
- vivid 生動程度　★★★★★★★★☆
- pertinent 切題度　★★★★★★☆☆☆

A reunion

I would like to talk about my elementary school's reunion. When I graduated from the elementary school, Facebook or other social media networks were not popular at that time. We still used traditional ways to contact each other, so it was difficult to keep in touch with my old classmates. One day I bumped into an old classmate on the street ten years after I graduated from the elementary

同學會

我想要談我國小的同學會。當我國小畢業時，Facebook或其他的社交網路並不普及。我們還是使用傳統的方式與同學聯絡，這樣使得聯繫上十分地困難。有一天，我在路上遇見了一位小學同學，當時已距離小學畢業十年了。我倆久別重逢，並開心地在一間咖啡館敘舊。

暖身話題
休閒話題
生活話題
常考話題
生活話題

school. We were very happy and had a chat at a café. She said she wanted to organise a group on Facebook to reunite with other old classmates. I thought it was a brilliant idea and tried to help her to contact some classmates I kept in touch with.

After a few months, we almost got in touch with all the classmates who accessed facebook. We announced that we were going to hold a reunion in three months. Most classmates who received the message on Facebook participated in the reunion. The venue was in a local restaurant. During the reunion, we talked about what we had been doing in the past decade. Some of my classmates went abroad, some of them got married and had children, and some of them started their own businesses. It was very interesting to see my classmates and find out what they had been up to. The reunion went very well. Thanks to a social media network, we reunited with old classmates.

她當時提到我們可以在Facebook上建立一個國小同學的群組,以利聯繫舊同學。我當時覺得這是一個很不錯的主意,便主動幫忙她聯絡一些我所知道的同學。

幾個月後,我們幾乎聯絡到大部分有使用Facebook的同學。我們在Facebook上公佈將在三個月後舉辦一場同學會,大部分收到訊息的同學皆出席。同學會的場地為一間當地的餐廳。在同學會上,我們聊起過去的十年來所發生的事情。有些同學出國,有些同學結婚生子,有些則自行創業。能和同學聊近況十分地有趣。同學會的進展很順利,也感謝社交網絡的幫助,讓我們與舊同學重逢。

💬 話題拓展

★ **Reunion** 同學會
★ **Traditional ways** 傳統方式
★ **Social media networks** 社交網絡
★ **Café** 咖啡館
★ **Local restaurants** 當地的餐廳
★ **Decade** 十年
★ **Venue** 舉辦地點

Notes

暖身話題
休閒話題
生活話題
常考話題
生活話題

「生活話題」

Rules of Engagement — A business you want to run

影集內容敘述

　　Audrey將工作辭去後，一直想找些事來打發時間。某日，她在地下室倉庫發現了一本奶奶留下來的餅乾食譜，就按照食譜做了些餅乾，請鄰居們試吃。沒想到這些餅乾大受歡迎。鄰居們正面的鼓勵，給了她信心，並激起了她開店做生意的念頭。然而，她的丈夫Jeff卻極力反對，原因是他認為更有生意頭腦的人都可能失敗，他不想她去冒險。兩人吵完架後，不歡而散。Jeff出外散心後，考慮了一會兒，決定支持老婆。他租下了一間店鋪，以利她籌備新的事業。

影集語彙

Burst into flames

- 釋 突然起火
- 例 Two cars crashed and burst into flames.
- 中 兩台車互撞後，就突然起火。

Rise and Shine

- 釋 快起床
- 例 It's seven o'clock. Rise and shine!
- 中 已經七點了，快起床。

Start-up

- 釋 剛起步的小公司
- 例 Jane runs a start-up and has been looking for new clients.
- 中 Jane成立了一間新的公司，努力地開拓新客源。

The pros and cons

- 釋 贊成和反對的理由
- 例 They debated the pros and cons of adopting a child.
- 中 他們在辯論領養小孩的利弊。

Figure out something

- 釋 弄明白；想出
- 例 Can you figure out the answer to this riddle?
- 中 你想出謎語的解答了嗎?

延伸話題

Breadwinner

Breadwinner originally means the person who brings bread home, so the family can continue surviving. It means the person who earns money that a family needs nowadays.

養家活口的人

Breadwinner字面上的意思為贏得麵包回家的人，延伸為賺錢養家活口的人。

Lease

A lease is a legal agreement to grant the use of a property, land, equipment or services for a specific time. In general, the legal owner of the asset is expected to receive regular rental payments.

租約

Lease為一種法律合約，指在特定期間內將房屋、土地、設備、或服務租讓給他人。一般而言，資產持有者會由承租方收到固定的租金收入。

🚲 **作者給力回答**　💿 MP3-21

- copious 豐富度　★★★★★★★★★☆
- creative 創意度　★★★★★★★☆☆☆
- impressive 深刻度　★★★★★★★★☆☆
- vivid 生動程度　★★★★★★★★★☆
- pertinent 切題度　★★★★★★☆☆☆

Describe a business you want to run

When I was in my early twenties, I wanted to run a ferry service. My hometown is a popular tourist attraction, which attracts thousands of tourists every day. Since many visitors come to admire beautiful river and mountain views, I thought it would be a great idea to run a ferry service on the river. However, my family didn't approve of this idea. They thought I was still young and did not want me to take risks. I was only twenty something at that time and didn't have much money. Due to

想經營的生意

當我二十初頭時，我曾想過要經營一個渡輪生意。我的家鄉是一個熱門的觀光景點，每天都吸引上千名的人潮。由於觀光客主要是到這觀賞山明水秀的風景，經營渡輪生意也許是一個不錯的主意。然而，我的父母並不贊成這門生意。他們覺得我還年輕，並不想我冒任何的風險。我當時僅二十初頭，手頭並沒有多餘的資金。也因如此，我無法完

暖身話題
休閒話題
生活話題
常考話題
生活話題

the lack of funds, I didn't start the ferry service business.

After a few years, there were a lot of ferries running across the river. It seems like it was a good business model because it brings a lot of competition on the river. It was a pity that we missed an opportunity. I think there are the pros and cons to running a business, you could be successful, but you have to take risks. For example, you would face fierce competition after other people try to emulate your business model. Some of my friends had startup companies and they worked very hard to get their products into the market. Some of the businesses went well. Some of the businesses went downhill and even went bust after a few years. I think taking risks and facing failures are important when learning to run a business.

成經營渡輪生意的夢想。

幾年後,水面上多了許多渡輪服務。許多同行加入競爭行列,這似乎是一個不錯的經營模式。當時失去了這個機會實在很可惜。我認為經營生意有好有壞,也許某些生意會成功,但須承擔風險。比如說,在別人學習你的商業模式後,你將會面臨嚴峻的競爭挑戰。我有些朋友自行創業,他們十分努力地將其產品推廣到市場上。其中一些朋友的企業經營的很成功,但另一些人的企業就每況愈下,甚至在幾年後破產。我認為承擔風險及面對失敗是學習經營生意中重要的一環。

話題拓展

★ **Ferry** 渡輪
★ **Hometown** 家鄉
★ **A popular tourist attraction** 熱門的觀光景點
★ **Opportunity** 機會
★ **The pros and cons** 優點及缺點
★ **Start-up** 剛起步的企業
★ **Run a business** 經營生意

Notes

Melissa & Joey — A surprise you had in your life

🌲 影集內容敘述

　　熱心的Melissa協助一位對婚禮事務不熟悉的朋友籌備婚禮。然而，她的朋友卻在婚禮舉行的前一個月宣布取消。原因是她的未婚夫向她坦承另有一段婚姻。由於婚禮在即，她不想讓幾個月來的努力前功盡棄，心想可否把此婚宴讓給其他的準新人，或許她與熱戀中的Joey可以用到這個現成的婚宴。她向Joey提議，但Joey覺得太突然，並沒有給她正面的回覆。然而，他卻祕密地計劃著給她一個意外的求婚驚喜。

🚗 影集語彙

Get cold feet

釋 臨陣退縮

例 The bride got the cold feet before the wedding and called it off.

中 新娘在婚禮前突然臨陣退縮，並取消婚禮。

Old school

釋 舊式的；老派的

例 Grandma prefers to keep the old school ideas.

中 奶奶傾向維持舊的觀念。

Lavish

釋 奢華的；慷慨的

例 The wedding was lavish with an endless supply of food and drinks.

中 這個婚宴很奢華，提供著無限供應的食物及飲品。

Fortune

釋 一大筆錢；一大筆財產

例 This house costs her a fortune.

中 這棟房子花了她一大筆錢。

Mess up

釋 弄糟；弄亂

> 例 Susan was unhappy because Ben messed up the room.
> 中 Susan很不高興，因為Ben把房間弄亂。

🎈 延伸話題

Caterer

A caterer is a person or company providing food and drink services at parties or functions. Catering services are very popular in Europe. Catering services can be seen in a variety of occasions, such as company meetings, weddings, social events, parties, and so on.

承辦酒席及宴會餐飲的公司

Caterer為承辦酒席及宴會餐飲的公司。宴會餐飲服務在歐洲非常地流行。在各式各樣的場合隨處可見宴會餐飲服務，如公司會議、婚宴、社交活動、派對等。

Accordionist

An accordionist is a person who plays a box-shaped keyboard musical instrument. An accordionist usually plays at restaurants or social events. It is popular to invite accordionists to play music during proposals.

手風琴家

手風琴家所演奏的樂器為附有鍵盤的箱式風琴。手風琴家經常在餐廳、及一些社交場合中演奏。目前很盛行在求婚過程中邀請手風琴家來演奏。

 作者給力回答 🔘 MP3-22

- **copious** 豐富度 ★★★★★★★★★☆
- **creative** 創意度 ★★★★★★☆☆☆
- **impressive** 深刻度 ★★★★★★★★☆☆
- **vivid** 生動程度 ★★★★★★★★★☆
- **pertinent** 切題度 ★★★★★★★☆☆☆

A surprise you had in your life

A surprise I had in my life was an electrical piano my parents gave me. When I was a teenager, I was interested in music and wanted to learn the piano. I didn't tell my parents that I wanted to learn to play the piano. When I passed by music shops, I always looked at the piano displayed in the window. I enjoyed going to a piano bar and listening to

人生中的驚喜

我人生中的一個驚喜是父母給我的一台電子琴。當我還是青少年時，我熱衷於音樂，並想學習鋼琴。但我並沒有告訴我的父母我想學鋼琴。每當經過樂器行時，我總是會朝展示窗的鋼琴望去。我也喜歡到鋼琴酒吧，聆聽現場音樂。我猜我的父母

the live music. I guess my parents noticed that I wanted to learn piano after observing my behaviour. They invited a piano salesman to our home and introduced some models they were selling. I was very surprised when I heard that my parents were thinking about me and going to buy me a piano. I had a look at the piano catalogue and chose an electrical piano.

The piano company delivered an electrical piano to my house a few days later. I was excited, and ran to the local bookstore and bought some piano music books. I realised that I had to hire a teacher because a musical novice can't read a piano music book. So my parents hired a piano teacher to teach me basic music theory for around two years. After I learned how to read the music books, I started to play the piano by myself. When I am tired or depressed, I play the piano. I felt relaxed after playing

因這些行為，注意到我想要學習鋼琴。他們請鋼琴銷售人員到家來為我介紹鋼琴種類。當時我十分的驚喜，因我的父母為我著想，並想買台鋼琴給我。我瀏覽了鋼琴目錄，並選了一台電子琴。

約幾天後，鋼琴公司運送了電子琴到我的家裡。我剛收到電子琴時，我十分地興奮，並跑到附近的書店買琴譜。我突然發現我不懂樂理，需要請一名鋼琴老師來教我樂理。我的父母請了一名鋼琴老師來教我學習約兩年的基本的樂理。在我能讀樂理時，我開始自學自彈。當我疲累或沮喪時，我會藉由彈琴來舒緩壓力。我想要向我的父母道

a few songs. I want to say thank you to my parents for buying me an electrical piano, so I can enjoy playing and listening to music.

謝，謝謝他們買了一台電子琴給我，我才能享受音樂。

💬 話題拓展

★ **Electrical piano** 電子琴
★ **Teenagers** 青少年
★ **Music shop** 樂器行
★ **Salesman** 銷售人員
★ **Piano music books** 琴譜
★ **Catalogue** 目錄
★ **Bookstore** 書店

Rules of Engagement — A neighbour

 **影集內容敘述**

　　在某次聚會上，Audrey無意向Liz透露她住的那間大廈樓上有間公寓要分租。沒想到，Liz真的租下那間公寓成為她的鄰居。自從她搬進來後，Audrey及Jeff夫妻倆就常聽到吵雜的音樂聲及敲打聲。Liz也三不五時地跑來串門子，使得兩夫妻完全沒有私人的生活。為了躲避Liz的騷擾，Audrey特意地關閉屋內所有的燈光，並減低音量，就為了讓Liz以為他們不在家，甚至還逃到其他鄰居家中躲藏。

🚗 影集語彙

Cut short

釋 縮短；打斷

例 Sorry that I have to cut you short.

中 對不起，我要打斷一下。

Sublet

釋 分租，轉租

例 I sublet my flat to get more revenue.

中 我將房子分租以取得更多收入。

Whereabouts

釋 下落；行蹤；在哪裡

例 David went missing for many days. His whereabouts are still unknown.

中 David失蹤多日，他的行蹤依然不明。

Miss out

釋 錯失機會

例 You don't want to miss out on the Christmas sales. This is the biggest sale during the year.

中 你不會想錯失聖誕特賣。這是一年之中最大的特賣活動。

Chicken out

釋 因害怕而放棄

> **例** Sean was going to ride a roller coaster but he chickened out.
>
> **中** Sean本來想玩雲霄飛車，但因害怕而放棄了。

 **延伸話題**

Housewarming

Housewarming is a party that people celebrate moving into a new home. This is an opportunity for house owners to show their new homes. Guests who attend the party usually bring gifts to furnish their new home.

喬遷慶祝

Housewarming為慶祝搬進新家的派對。屋主藉著這個機會來展示他們的新家。而賓客們也會贈送禮物給搬進新家的屋主。

Tap Dance

When dancers perform tap dance, they wear shoes fitted with metal taps and make a rhythmic sound on the floor.

踢踏舞

當舞者在表演踢踏舞時，穿著附有金屬片的踢踏舞鞋，拍擊地板並發出有節奏的聲音。

作者給力回答　🄫 MP3-23

- **copious 豐富度**　★★★★★★★★★☆
- **creative 創意度**　★★★★★★☆☆☆
- **impressive 深刻度**　★★★★★★★☆☆
- **vivid 生動程度**　★★★★★★★★☆
- **pertinent 切題度**　★★★★★★☆☆☆

A neighbour

Due to my job relocation, I have lived in many different places. Most of my neighbours had busy lives and did not really talk much. However, one of my neighbours was very helpful and warm-hearted. She was around thirty something and had been living in the building for around two years with her husband and her son. When I just moved in, I didn't know anything about our neighbourhood. She was willing to tell me everything she knew and showed me around the area. Since she had been living in this area for two years, she knew some

鄰居

由於外派工作的關係，我住過許多不同的地方。大部分的鄰居都十分忙碌，且很少來往。然而，其中的一位鄰居十分地友善及熱心。她大約三十多歲，與老公和兒子住在這棟大樓約兩年。當我剛搬進來時，對於陌生的週遭一無所知。她總是很樂意地告訴我她所知道的事，也會帶我到附近逛逛。由於她已經住在這個區域兩年，她熟悉附近的公園及商店。我們曾在天

暖身話題

休閒話題

生活話題

常考話題

生活話題

good parks and shops in the neighbourhood. We used to take a walk in a nearby park or go to a café when the weather was nice. She also invited me to her house for a cup of tea when we were free.

When I had a housewarming party, she came around and prepared some snacks. In order to say thank you to her, I invited her for dinner. It is not easy to find an amiable neighbour like her nowadays because most people are busy with their lives. I heard a lot of stories about annoying neighbours, but I was very lucky to have her as a neighbour. I lived in that building for two years and moved to a bigger place. When I am free, I still drop in on her. She still tells me what happens in our neighbourhood as usual.

氣好時，一同散步到鄰近的公園或咖啡館。空閒時，她也邀請我到她家喝茶。

當我舉行喬遷慶宴時，她會到我家幫我準備一些點心。我也招待她晚餐，以答謝她的幫忙。由於大部分的人皆忙於生計，現在的社會很難找到像她這麼友善的鄰居。我也聽說許多惡鄰居的故事，但我很幸運能有一個好鄰居。我在那棟大樓住了兩年，便搬到更寬敞的地方。當我有空時，我依然會順道拜訪她。她還是像往常一樣，把她所知道鄰近地區的事告訴我。

💬 話題拓展

★ **Job relocation** 工作調動
★ **Thirtysomething** 三十多歲的人
★ **Neighbourhood** 鄰近地區
★ **Housewarming party** 喬遷慶宴
★ **Parks and shops in the neighbourhood** 鄰近的公園或咖啡館
★ **Snacks** 點心
★ **Annoying neighbours** 討厭的鄰居

Notes

My family — A teacher in your childhood

🌿 影集內容敘述

　　Kenzo向其叔叔Michael抱怨，他的美術老師Mr. Tilley給了他的美術作品非常低的分數。Michael回憶起小時也上過Mr. Tilley的美術課，淘氣的他時常捉弄Mr. Tilley。Michael認為Kenzo美術拿低分，可能為Mr. Tilley的報復行為。他親自到學校找Mr. Tilley幫Kenzo求情，但當Mr. Tilley提到他最近發現Michael當學生時尚有作業未交，Michael就嚇得逃跑了。當Kenzo得知此事後，取笑Michael懦弱，Michael決定再赴學校找Mr. Tilley談判。然而，Mr. Tilley表示他給Kenzo低分並非任何報復行為，並把Kenzo的作品給Michael看。但Michael看過姪子的作品後，便認為Mr. Tilley給的分數十分的公平。

影集語彙

Prank
釋 惡作劇
例 Kids like to play pranks on teacher.
中 小孩子喜歡對老師惡作劇。

Hand in
釋 提交；繳交
例 Have you handed in your report?
中 你繳交報告了沒?

On an equal footing
釋 站在平等的地位
例 People from different ethnic backgrounds should compete for jobs on an equal footing.
中 不同膚色的人種在求職上應站在平等的地位。

Head over heels in love
釋 墜入情網
例 Kelly and Richard are head over heels in love with each other.
中 Kelly和Richard彼此互相深愛著對方。

Peace of mind
釋 安心；放心

例 For her peace of mind, she run home to check if she turned off the gas.

中 她得回家確認瓦斯有關好才放心。

延伸話題

Primary school

Primary school is a school where school kids receive elementary education. A primary school is a compulsory education for children from the ages of around five to ten in the United Kingdom.

小學

小學是學童接受基本教育的地方。在英國，接受強制性小學教育的年齡層為五到十歲。

Detention

Detention is a type of punishment for school kids. They stay at school for a short time after the classes have finished.

放學後留堂

Detention為一種懲罰學童的方式。放學後，學童留守在學校幾個小時作為懲罰。

作者給力回答　MP3-24

- copious 豐富度　★★★★★★★★☆
- creative 創意度　★★★★★★☆☆☆
- impressive 深刻度　★★★★★★★★☆
- vivid 生動程度　★★★★★★★★☆
- pertinent 切題度　★★★★★★☆☆☆

A teacher in my childhood

　　I met many different teachers in my academic life, but Mr. Lin was an important teacher who had an influence on my life. Mr. Lin originally taught in another school and he was transferred to our school in my last year of the elementary school. He taught us Chinese. When I studied at elementary school, I didn't perform very well academically. I guess that I just didn't know how to study effectively.

　　He encouraged students to read more extracurricular books and attend

兒童時期的老師

　　在我的學習生涯中，遇過了不少老師。其中林老師是影響我人生的一位重要的老師。林老師原本在其他學校任教，他是在我小學的最後一年轉來我們的學校，並在我們的班級教中文。當我讀小學時，學業表現並不好。我猜我當時並不懂得有效地學習。

　　他鼓勵學生應多讀一些課外讀物，並參加一些

暖身話題

休閒話題

生活話題

常考話題

生活話題

153

more outdoor activities. I still remember that he recommended a few books for us to read during the summer vacation. I read the books he recommended and thought these books were useful for school kids. I learnt some good vocabulary from reading these books, which helped my Chinese writing skills.

I wasn't good at maths at that time. He recommended a maths tutor for me. My maths improved significantly after I had a maths tutor. Before I met Mr. Lin, I didn't know how to study and wasn't interested in studying. However, he changed my life. He made me feel that I could achieve anything if I found the right method. If I hadn't met him and listened to his advice, I would probably still have struggled with studying. I appreciated his help and thought he was a great teacher. My life was better because of his help.

戶外活動。我記得他推薦了一些於暑期閱讀的書籍。我讀了他推薦的這些書後，覺得對學童的幫助很大。我從中學習到很多實用的字彙，並加強了我的中文寫作能力。

我當時的數學並不好。他推薦了一位數學家教。我的數學能力也因這位家教的指導下進步神速。在我認識林老師前，並不懂得如何讀書，甚至對讀書沒有興趣。然而，他改變了我的人生，並讓我覺得只要找對了方法，就能達成某目標。我很感謝他的幫助並覺得他是一個好老師，我的人生因他的幫助而更順利。

💬 話題拓展

★ **My academic life** 我的學術生涯
★ **Extracurricular books** 課外讀物
★ **Outdoor activities** 戶外活動
★ **Summer vacation** 暑假
★ **School kids** 學童
★ **Vocabulary** 字彙

Notes

My family — An old thing in your family

🍃 影集內容敘述

　　Janey和Michael突然提議將招待父母出國旅遊，做為父母結婚紀念日的禮物。兩人其實心裡已打定主意父母根本不可能會成行，因為父母之前共同旅遊時有一些不愉快的回憶。沒想到，父母考慮後，竟然答應成行。Michael情急之下，先用信用卡支付旅費。當父母出國後，兩人開始急忙地想辦法籌錢支付旅費。他們想到以變賣家中古董的方式，籌措現金。她請了一位古董專家到家中鑑價。沒想到，家中除了一個古董鐘外，無一值錢的物品。但這個鐘是他們的母親最喜歡的一個古董。在想不出更好的對策下，兩人還是將這個古董鐘拍賣掉了。然而，當父母回到家時，他們告知因旅途過程中發生了一些意外，他們獲得三千英鎊的賠償金，這筆錢剛好足以支付旅費。Janey和Michael這時才後悔莫及，草率地賣掉母親最喜愛的古董鐘。

影集語彙

Stand on one's own two feet

釋 獨立；自立

例 Jenny has reached thirty this year. She should be able to stand on her own feet.

中 Jenny已經三十歲了，她應該有能力自立了。

Spread your wings

釋 展翅高飛

例 Louise has just finished university. It is time to spread her wings.

中 Louise剛剛大學畢業，這是她展翅高飛的時刻。

Force of habit

釋 出於習慣

例 It's force of habit that I wake up at five o'clock every morning.

中 出於習慣，我每天早上五點起床。

In the first place

釋 起初；最初

例 If he still owed us money, we should not lend him money in the first place.

中 他還是欠我們錢，我們最初就不該借錢給他。

暖身話題

休閒話題

生活話題

常考話題

生活話題

Outbreak

釋 突然暴發的疾病

例 The recent outbreak has killed hundreds of people.

中 最近暴發的疾病已經造成上百名的死亡案例。

 **延伸話題**

Auction

In general, an auction is a public sale of goods or property, where the highest bidder won the bid. Auctions have become very popular recently with many online auction platforms appearing in the market.

拍賣

Auction為一種公開的拍賣活動，拍賣標的可為物品或財產。一般而言，拍賣標的由出標最高者可獲得。拍賣在市場上已多年，也愈來愈普及。近年來網路拍賣平台也如雨後春筍般地迅速發展。

Reproduction

A reproduction is a copy of an artwork, such as paintings, sculptures, antiques and so on. Most reproductions are copies of paintings and artworks by famous artists.

複製品

Reproduction為藝術品的複製品，像是畫作、雕塑、及古董等。

大部分的複製品來自於知名藝術家的作品。

 作者給力回答　　MP3-25

- **copious** 豐富度　★★★★★★★★★☆
- **creative** 創意度　★★★★★★★☆☆☆
- **impressive** 深刻度　★★★★★★★★☆☆
- **vivid** 生動程度　★★★★★★★★★☆
- **pertinent** 切題度　★★★★★★★☆☆☆

An old thing in your family

　　An old thing in my family is a stamp album, which I inherited from my grandfather. Collecting stamps was popular for his generation. He started collecting stamps when he was twentysomething and had collected a variety of stamps. These stamps were about thirty years old. Since I am interested in collecting stamps, he gave them to me as a gift.

　　I like collecting stamps because

家裡的老舊物品

　　我們家中一個老舊的物品是一本集郵冊，這是從我爺爺那繼承而來的。集郵在過去很盛行。他從二十多歲時開始收集各式各樣的郵票，這本集郵冊已有三十年的歷史。因為我對集郵有興趣，他便將這本集郵冊送給我。

　　我喜歡集郵是因為郵

暖身話題

休閒話題

生活話題

常考話題

生活話題

159

stamps represent history, people, and places. They also have educational benefits because stamps tell stories, past events and celebrations which happened in the past. When I reviewed the stamps after a few years, it reminded of me what had happened in the world at that time. I like stamps with postmarks. When I go travelling, I usually buy local stamps and send letters home. When these letters arrive home, I can see the country and postmark dates. When I travelled to London, I bought a stamp from the British museum. I sent a letter home, so I could have a stamp with a British postmark on it.

I still collect stamps as a hobby. However, stamps are not commonly used nowadays due to the rise of the internet. People prefer to use e-mails and social media networks to deliver their messages. Traditional mail deliveries are not as popular as before. If stamps no longer exist in

票描繪出歷史、人物、及景點。它也富有教育的價值,因為郵票的背後訴説著過去發生的故事、事件、及慶祝活動。當我於多年後再次回顧這些郵票時,它提醒著我當時世界上所發生的事。我喜歡含有郵戳的郵票。當我旅遊時,我通常會買當地的郵票,並寄回家。當這些信抵達家裡時,就可以看見郵戳上的地點及日期。當我赴倫敦旅行時,我在大英博物館買了一枚郵票,並將它寄回家,所以我就可以保留英國的郵戳。

我還是將收藏郵票當做我的興趣。然而,由於網際網路的發達,郵票不是這麼普遍的被使用。現代人偏好使用電子郵件或社交網絡來傳達訊息。傳統的郵件傳遞已不再盛行。假如有一天郵票在世

the future, I will still browse them because they will remind me of the old hobby I had when I was young.

界上消失了，我還是會瀏覽它，因為它提醒著我，這是我年輕時曾有的一個興趣。

話題拓展

★ **A stamp album** 集郵冊
★ **History** 歷史
★ **People** 人物
★ **Places** 景點
★ **Educational benefits** 教育的價值
★ **Celebrations** 慶祝活動
★ **Postmarks** 郵戳
★ **The British museum** 大英博物館

Rules of Engagement — A person you know who speaks a different language

🌿 影集內容敘述

　　Russell遇見了一名俏麗的義大利女郎，並邀請她共進晚餐。因他不諳義大利語，他請精通義大利語的助理Timmy協助翻譯。Timmy雖然盡力幫忙翻譯，但他實在受不了Russell開門見山的提問方式。Timmy提醒他第一次約會應該收斂些，Russell勉強答應才問一些初次約會常問的問題。兩人談得甚歡，並相約續攤。然而，經過一夜的相處後，Russell覺得這名義大利女郎並不適合他，想請Timmy翻譯並打發她走。Timmy對於Russell的行徑十分不悅。他故意不照他的意思翻譯，讓該名女郎誤以為Russell對她有意。

🚗 影集語彙

Loaded

釋 有錢的

例 They bought a detached house in the central London with cash. They must be loaded.

中 他們在倫敦市中心用現金買了一間獨棟房子，他們應該很富裕。

Rusty

釋 荒廢的；生疏的（對於知識或能力）

例 I haven't got a chance to practice my Japanese. It's a bit rusty now.

中 我已經好久沒有練習日文，現在已經有些生疏了。

Hang around with somebody

釋 與某人廝混

例 I don't want you hang around with him because he might be a criminal.

中 我不想你跟他廝混，因他可能是罪犯。

Triumph

釋 大勝利

例 The governing party achieved a triumph in the election.

中 執政黨在選舉中大獲全勝。

暖身話題

休閒話題

生活話題

常考話題

生活話題

Clingy

釋 易黏人的

例 Jean was a clingy child when she was young.

中 Jean小時候喜歡黏著人。

 延伸話題

Study abroad

Studying abroad is when students leave their home countries and take courses in different countries. Studying abroad has become popular for young people nowadays. The benefits of studying abroad are to learn languages, experiencing different cultures, seeing the world, making friends from around the world, becoming independent and so on.

海外留遊學

海外留遊學為學生離開原本定居的國家，遠赴海外求學。近年來，海外留遊學愈來愈盛行。海外留遊學的好處為學習外語、體驗異國文化、開拓國際視野、結交國際朋友、學習獨立自主等。

Language exchange

Language exchange is a way to practice a foreign language with a language partner who speaks a language you intend to learn. In general, a face to face language exchange is helpful for language learning especially in speaking and listening.

On the other hand, learning by e-mails or social media networks can help to improve writing and reading. Students usually find a language exchange partner in language schools and universities.

語言交換

　　語言交換為兩個不同的語言學習者透過學習對方母語，來增進彼此的外語能力。一般而言，面對面的語言交換有助於口說及聽力。而透過E-mails、或社交平台的語言交換，則有助於寫作及閱讀。學生通常透過語言學校及大學來找語言交換對象。

 作者給力回答　MP3-26

- **copious 豐富度**　★★★★★★★★★☆
- **creative 創意度**　★★★★★★★☆☆☆
- **impressive 深刻度**　★★★★★★★★☆☆
- **vivid 生動程度**　★★★★★★★★★☆
- **pertinent 切題度**　★★★★★★★☆☆☆

A person you know who speaks a different language

　　A person I know who speaks a different language is one of my German friends. He speaks fluent Mandarin Chinese. I was amazed by

說外語的朋友

　　我想要談我認識的一位德國朋友。他講著流利的中文。當我們初次見面時，我對他流利的中文大

暖身話題　休閒話題　生活話題　常考話題　生活話題

his Chinese when I first met him. Not a lot of foreigners can speak fluent Chinese unless they were born and raised in a Chinese speaking country. He had been learning Chinese for more than ten years and had lived in China for a couple of years. He told me that he also read Chinese newspapers on the train in the morning. Since Chinese reading is harder than speaking Chinese, I guess he must have put a lot of effort into his studies. His language skills also helped him to get a job in Shanghai.

He is also learning Korean now. As an Asian language speaker, I find it difficult enough to learn an Asian language not to mention a different language family. I asked him if it's difficult to learn so many Asian languages. He told me that most regional languages have similar rules, it is not hard to learn many different regional languages at the same time. I guess that he must be interested in

為驚奇。除非在華語的環境下成長，很少有外籍人士能說流利的中文。他學習中文已超過十年的時間，並也在中國住了幾年。他告訴我他早晨搭火車時，也會在火車上閱讀中文報紙。由於中文閱讀比口說還難，我猜他應該下了不少功夫在中文學習上。他的中文能力也幫助他在上海找到一份工作。

他目前也在學習韓語中。作為一個亞洲語系的母語人士，我覺得韓語挺難學的，何況是一位歐語人士。我問他學習這麼多的亞洲語言是否困難，他說大部分的區域性的語言有相似的規則，同時學起來並不困難。我猜他一定很喜愛亞洲文化及語言，才能精通這些語言。我目

Asian cultures and languages to master these languages. I plan to learn an Asian language and asked him about tips for learning Asian languages. His advice was very helpful and I picked up another Asian language quickly.

前也打算學習一種亞洲語言，便向他請教一些學習亞洲語系的方法。他的建議十分地受用，我也很快地掌握學習亞洲語言的訣竅。

💬 話題拓展

★ **German friends** 德國朋友
★ **Fluent Mandarin Chinese** 流利的中文
★ **Chinese newspapers** 中文報紙
★ **Language skills** 語言能力
★ **Foreigners** 外籍人士
★ **Similar rules** 相似的規則
★ **Korean** 韓語

暖身話題
休閒話題
生活話題
常考話題
生活話題

The Big Bang Theory — A TV programme you love

🌲 影集內容敘述

　　Sheldon最喜愛的電視節目無預警地停播了，他氣沖沖地打電話到電視台抱怨，卻沒有下文。Amy認為Sheldon患有強迫性完成每件事情的心理障礙，決定要幫助他克服這個障礙。她準備了幾個練習活動，像是她故意不把話講完，而去做別的事。她讓Sheldon玩井字遊戲，在他快贏時，就讓遊戲草草結束。她讓Sheldon吹熄生日蛋糕上的蠟燭，卻故意遮住其中一支蠟燭，不讓他吹熄全部蠟燭。在經歷好幾個遊戲後，Sheldon告知Amy他覺得好多了，但事實上他只是想打發她走，他還是無法跳脫這個心理障礙。在她走後，Sheldon獨自完成所有剛剛未結束的遊戲。

影集語彙

Passionate about something

釋 非常喜愛某事

例 Simon is passionate about tennis.

中 Simon非常喜愛打網球。

Weirdo

釋 怪人；怪物

例 Since he behaves strangely, all the other classmates called him a weirdo.

中 由於他表現怪異，其他的同學叫他怪人。

Creepy

釋 令人毛骨悚然的

例 I don't like that creepy TV programme.

中 我不喜歡那個令人毛骨悚然的電視節目。

As a rule

釋 一般來說；通常

例 As a rule, Cindy doesn't take sugar in coffee.

中 Cindy通常喝咖啡不加糖。

Pitch in

釋 動手做；齊心協力

例 After a typhoon, people always pitch in and rebuild their

homes.

 颱風過後，總是能看見群眾一同齊心協力重整家園。

 延伸話題

Tic-tac-toe

Tic-tac-toe is a paper and pencil game played by two people. Each player takes turns and writes either X or O in a pattern of nine squares. The winner is the first player who places three Xs or three Os in a horizontal, vertical, or diagonal straight line.

井字遊戲

井字遊戲為一種兩人合玩的紙筆遊戲。每個玩家輪流在一個井字方格中畫X和O。贏家為首先將三個X或O排列成水平列、垂直列、或對角線列者。

Cliffhanger

A cliffhanger is a suspenseful ending in a film or an episode of a serial. The purpose of a cliffhanger is to make audience to return to see the next episode.

扣人心弦的結局

Cliffhanger為在電影或電視連續劇結尾時，特意製造出一些緊張刺激的情節，以讓觀眾能返回再觀賞下集的內容。

作者給力回答　　MP3-27

- **copious** 豐富度　★★★★★★★★★☆
- **creative** 創意度　★★★★★★★☆☆☆
- **impressive** 深刻度　★★★★★★★★☆☆
- **vivid** 生動程度　★★★★★★★★★☆
- **pertinent** 切題度　★★★★★★☆☆☆

A TV programme you love

My favourite TV programme is a British reality TV show. Each show invites four to five people to host competing dinner parties for each other. Each participant will rate the host's overall performance. At the end of the week, the contestant with the highest score will win the competition. In order to win the competition, each contestant really bends over backwards to impress the other people.

The reasons why I enjoy watching this show is because I can

喜愛的電視節目

我最喜歡的電視節目是一個英國的真人電視秀。它每集都會邀請四到五位的參賽者，為彼此舉辦晚宴，每位參賽者會互相評論對方的總體表現。在每週結束，獲得最高分數的參賽者將會贏得比賽。每位參賽者竭盡全力地準備晚宴，希望能留給賓客一個好的印象，以贏得比賽。

我喜歡這個節目的原因是，我可以從中學習到

learn cooking from contestants. They usually cook international cuisine and have some secret recipes to impress other guests. Another reason I like this show is I can have a understanding about British lifestyle and cultures from this programme. People attending this show are blunt in their comments about the other host's dinner. They usually say what they think and don't care they are on the TV.In the most unforgettable episode I have seen, two contestants had an argument because they didn't like each other's personalities. Neither of them won the competition.

On the other hand, some of my friends don't like this programme. They think this is a low budget TV programme. This programme doesn't have to hire a host or actors and just invite ordinary people to host dinner parties. My friends prefer to watch action films with complicated plots. Although some people don't like this

烹飪的技巧。參賽者通常煮國際料理,並準備一些使賓客印象深刻的秘密食譜。另一個喜歡這個節目的理由是,我可以從中了解到英國的生活及文化。參加這個節目的參賽者皆十分地直率。他們通常會直接表達所想的,也不會在乎他們在上節目。我印象最深的一集是,兩個參賽者因彼此不喜歡對方的個性,而大吵一架。結果,兩人都與獎無緣。

從另一個角度來看,我的一些朋友們就不喜歡這個節目。他們覺得這是一個低成本的電視節目。這個節目不需請主持人或演員,僅需邀請一般民眾來舉辦晚宴。而我的朋友們偏好看有複雜情節的動作片。雖然有些人不喜歡

programme, it's very popular in the UK. I guess hosting a dinner party is a part of British culture and viewers want to know what other people do when they host dinner parties.

這個節目，但它在英國是非常地受歡迎。我猜舉辦晚宴是英國文化的一環，而觀眾們想要藉此了解其他人如何舉行晚宴。

話題拓展

★ **Reality TV show** 真人秀
★ **Overall performance** 總體表現
★ **Contestants** 參賽者
★ **Host** 主持人
★ **A low budget TV programme** 低成本的電視節目
★ **Action films with complicated plots** 有複雜情節的動作片
★ **Plot** 情節

Friends — A house

🌲 影集內容敘述

　　Rachel和Phoebe發現Chandler和一名美麗的金髮女郎一同驅車前往紐約郊區的一間房子，並單獨相處了四十五分鐘。Rachel和Phoebe以為他們倆人有姦情，趕緊告知Monica這個消息。事實上，Monica和Chandler正準備買屋。這名金髮女郎為一名房仲，Chandler和她是一同相約看屋。Rachel一行人得知實情後，十分地驚訝。想起過去一同當鄰居的美好回憶，一夥人十分地不捨。然而，Monica和Chandler已決定搬離紐約，以給領養的孩子更好的生活環境。倆人當時已出價，正等待屋主的回覆。Chandler突然接到一通房仲打來的電話，屋主已接受他們的出價。但為了不讓朋友們傷心，Chandler暫時隱瞞了這個消息。

影集語彙

Underpriced

釋 低於市價的

例 Since the seller is desperate to sell his house, its house is underpriced.

中 由於屋主急著脫手，這間房子的要價低於市價。

Homey

釋 像家一樣的舒適

例 This country cottage is so homey. I want to stay here for holiday.

中 這個鄉村小屋像家一樣的舒適，我好想到這渡假。

Make an offer

釋 出價；開價

例 The asking price for this house was £200,000. We made an offer of £195,500.

中 這間房子的要價為200,000英鎊，我們的開價為195,500英鎊。

Swing set

釋 鞦韆

例 This house comes with a swing set. It is suitable for families with children

中 這橦房子附有一套鞦韆，非常適合有兒童的家庭。

Neighbourhood

釋 鄰近地區；街坊；住宅區

例 This couple has been looking for a good neighbourhood to raise their children.

中 這對夫妻一直在找尋適合他們孩子生長的住宅區。

 延伸話題

Realtor

A realtor's job is to arrange house viewings, buy and sell properties, manage homes, land and buildings for their clients. The term realtor is commonly used in the United States, and the term real estate agent is commonly used in the United Kingdom.

房地產經紀人

Realtor的工作主要為安排客戶看房，買賣房子交易，為客戶管理房屋、土地及大樓等事宜。Realtor為美國通用的說法。英國則稱作Real estate agent。

Attic

An attic is a room on the top of a building, and just under the roof, especially for a detached house or a semi-detached house. An attic is usually used for storage.

閣樓

　　Attic介於屋子的最上層及屋頂之下，通常獨棟或雙併房子設有閣樓。它通常作為儲存物品之用。

作者給力回答　🔘 MP3-28

- **copious 豐富度**　★★★★★★★★★☆
- **creative 創意度**　★★★★★★☆☆☆
- **impressive 深刻度**　★★★★★★★★☆☆
- **vivid 生動程度**　★★★★★★★★☆
- **pertinent 切題度**　★★★★★★☆☆☆

A house

　　I'm going to talk about a house I viewed. I was looking for a family house with three to four bedrooms. I went to view a house near the seaside. It was a semi-detached house with a small pond in the garden. There was a living room, a kitchen, a dining room and a garden on the ground floor. It had a spacious master bedroom with a jacuzzi on the first floor. The guest

房屋

　　我要談我之前看過的一個房屋。我當時在找三到四房的房子，並到了一個臨近海邊的地區看屋。那是一棟附有池塘及花園的雙併住宅。一樓有一間客廳、一間廚房、一間餐廳、及一個庭園。二樓有一間附有按摩浴缸的寬敞主臥房。而客房及書房則

暖身話題　休閒話題　生活話題　常考話題　生活話題

bedrooms and an office were on the second floor. There was a massive balcony on the top floor, where you could see a beautiful sea view. There was a small bar next to the balcony, so you could grab a drink from the bar and admire the view from the balcony.

My favourite place in this house was its garden. It had a decent sized garden with a pond. You could plant flowers around the pond. I felt relaxed when I saw the garden from the living room. My brother's favorite floor of this house was its second floor. It had two guest rooms and an office. There was a large bookshelf in the office, so you could put hundreds of books on that bookshelf. Since my brother enjoys reading, this is an ideal place for him to study.

Moreover, there was a nice riverside pathway near the house. Whenever I got bored, I could go out

在三樓。頂樓有一個超大的露天陽台,你可以從陽台遠眺美麗的海景。在陽台旁邊有個小型的吧台,你可以從吧台取得飲料及觀賞海景。

我最喜歡的地方是它的庭園。它是一個附有池塘的寬廣的花園。你可以在池塘旁種植花草。每當我從客廳向庭園望去時,我就覺得十分地放鬆。我弟弟最喜歡的樓層是二樓,它有兩間客房及一間書房。書房裡有一個大型的書櫃,你可以放上百本書在書櫃裡。由於我的弟弟喜愛閱讀,這對他來說,是個理想的讀書環境。

此外,這棟房子附近有一個環河步道。當我無聊時,我可以直接出門,

at the drop of a hat and have a relaxing walk along the river. The only disadvantage is that this house was in the middle of nowhere. There were no shops around and you had to drive to get everywhere. Since we couldn't secure a mortgage, we didn't buy the house. However, it was my dream house. I hope that I can go back and view that house again.

並沿著河岸散步。這棟房子唯一的缺點是它的位置偏遠，附近沒有任何的商店，而且到哪都要以車代步。由於一些原因，我們並沒有買這棟房子。然而，這是我理想中的房子。我希望有朝一日我能再回去看那間房子。

💬 話題拓展

★ **Seaside** 海邊
★ **Semi-detached house** 雙併住宅
★ **Master bedroom** 主臥房
★ **Jacuzzi** 按摩浴缸
★ **Balcony** 陽台
★ **A decent size garden with a pond** 有池塘的寬廣的花園
★ **Ideal house** 理想中的房子

主題
29

Friends — Shopping

影集內容敘述

　　Ross準備去參加一個約會，並請愛好時尚的Rachel提供一些服裝建議。Rachel直言他買的那頂帽子，完全不搭配，並說她剛好要去購物，可以帶他去服裝店給他一些建議。到了服裝店後，Rachel為Ross選購一些適合約會的衣服。然而，他們卻拿錯彼此的購物袋。對服裝沒有概念的Ross，拿到Rachel買給自己的女性毛衣，便不以為意的穿出門。一路上，路人對他指指點點的，他卻以為自己的服裝品味吸引他人的目光。然而，到了約會地點後，發現約會對象也穿著同款的毛衣時，他才知道自己穿的是女性毛衣。他尷尬的草草結束這場約會。

🚗 影集語彙

All eyes are on somebody or something

釋 萬眾矚目

例 All eyes are on that celebrity who is having dinner in a restaurant.

中 在餐廳裡用餐的名人是萬眾矚目的焦點。

Go nuts

釋 暴跳如雷；發狂

例 Rebecca went nuts when she found out her wallet had been stolen.

中 當Rebecca發現她的錢包被偷時，整個人暴跳如雷。

Thoughtful

體貼的；考慮周到的

例 Jennifer is a thoughtful wife. She makes a lunch box for her husband everyday.

中 Jennifer是一位體貼的妻子。她每天幫她的老公準備午餐盒。

Tease

釋 戲弄

例 Calm down. She was only teasing.

中 冷靜點，她只是在戲弄你。

Intimidating

釋 嚇人的；令人生畏的

例 A job interview can be intimidating.

中 面試有時是令人生畏的。

 **延伸話題**

Anonymity

Anonymity is a situation when someone's name is not given or known.

匿名

匿名是指當某人的姓名不便提供或不知。

A shopping outlet

A shopping outlet is a retail store where manufacturers sell their stock directly to the public. A shopping outlet used to be attached to a factory in the past.

暢貨中心

暢貨中心是指原廠製造商直接將它們的庫存在商店賣給大眾。在過去，暢貨中心通常設在工廠旁邊。

作者給力回答　MP3-29

- copious 豐富度 ★★★★★★★★★☆
- creative 創意度 ★★★★★☆☆☆
- impressive 深刻度 ★★★★★★★☆☆
- vivid 生動程度 ★★★★★★★★☆
- pertinent 切題度 ★★★★★★☆☆☆

暖身話題　休閒話題　生活話題　常考話題　生活話題

Shopping Mall

I'd like to talk about my favourite shopping centre. It is about an hours drive from my house and I go there around every three months. It is an outlet shopping centre with hundreds of well-known brands. Each shop has a selection of products you can buy, such as clothes, home appliances, jewellery, watches, and shoes. I like to go shopping in this outlet shopping centre because there is a good selection of womenswear, and it is brilliant value for money. You can get designers' clothes at discount prices. It is best to arrive at the

購物中心

我想要談一個我喜愛的購物中心。它大約距離我家一個小時的車程，我大約每隔三個月去一次。它是擁有上百種知名品牌的暢貨中心。每個商店有各式各樣的商品可以選購，像是服飾、家電、珠寶、手錶、及鞋子。我喜歡到這個暢貨中心購物的原因是，它有許多女性服飾可供挑選，並且物超所值。你可以買到打折的設計師品牌服飾。到這個購物中心的最佳時段是早

shopping centre early in the morning because you can get a good parking space and there are fewer people queuing in the shops. There are some good cafés and restaurants in the shopping centre. You can take a break or have lunch at one of the cafés after shopping.

上，因為你可以找到好的停車位置，並且較少人在商店排隊。購物中心裡也有許多好的咖啡館及餐廳。逛累了也可以在咖啡館裡休息或用午餐。

It is also a popular tourist destination for international visitors. When I go there, it is always packed with tourists and tour buses. The best day to go shopping in this shopping centre is Boxing Day. You can get the best value for money on this day. However, the shopping centre can be very busy and crowded. If you don't like seeing a lot of shoppers, it might not be a good idea to go there on Boxing Day. I usually check its promotions or offers online before I visit the shopping centre, so I can make the most of my shopping and get products I want.

這裡也是一個海外觀光客嚮往的知名的景點。每次我到這個購物中心，總是隨處可見遊客及旅遊巴士。到此購物中心的最佳時間是聖誕節的次日。在這天，你可以購得十分划算的商品。然而，購物中心可能會人滿為患。假如你不喜歡看到擁擠的人潮，或許在聖誕節的次日赴購物中心不是一個好的主意。我通常會在赴購物中心前，先在網路上查詢促銷活動。如此，我可以將我的購物時間做最充分的利用。

話題拓展

★ **Favourite shopping centre** 喜愛的購物中心
★ **Outlet shopping centre** 暢貨中心
★ **Womenswear** 女裝
★ **Designers' clothes** 設計師品牌服飾
★ **Shopper** 購物者
★ **Promotion** 促銷活動
★ **A popular tourist destination for international visitors** 海外觀光客嚮往的知名的景點

Notes

Friends ─ Eating out

🌿 影集內容敘述

　　Joey看上了Phoebe的一名友人Sarah，並請Phoebe撮合他們倆人約會。Joey邀請Sarah到餐廳共進晚餐，倆人雖然聊的來，但Sarah有一個Joey忌諱的習慣，她常不由自主地伸手拿他餐盤裡的薯條。Joey非常討厭與人共食，對Sarah的初次印象也大大折扣。在Phoebe的努力勸說下，Joey決定再給Sarah一次機會，一同共享晚餐。這次他有備而來，他特別點了一份加大薯條，準備讓Sarah享用。然而，這次Sarah看上他餐盤裡的蛤蜊，又想伸手去拿。Joey終於忍受不了，告訴Sarah他介意與人共食。Sarah了解後，便不再伸手拿他的食物。上甜點時，Joey因他點的甜點不如預期，竟看上Sarah點的甜點，在她接電話離席時，將她的甜點全部吃完。Sarah對他的行徑十分地反感，約會也跟著告吹。

影集語彙

Out of nowhere

釋 突然

例 The robber came out of nowhere. David didn't even notice him.

中 強盜突然不知從哪冒出來，David甚至沒有注意到。

Set someone up with

釋 撮合某人

例 Phoebe tries to set Sarah up with Joey.

中 Phoebe想要撮合Sarah 和Joey。

On top of something

釋 掌握現況

例 Ian is the new project manager. He must stay on top of the project status.

中 Ian是新任的專案經理。他必須要掌握目前專案的現況。

Two-way street

釋 互諒互讓的關係

例 A relationship is a two-way street.

中 感情是互諒互讓的關係。

Overreact

釋 反應過度

> **例** She overreacts to this issue. It can be resolved easily.
> **中** 她對這件事反應過度，這事其實是很容易解決的。

 **延伸話題**

Shrimp cocktail

Shrimp cocktail is a seafood dish served in a glass. It contains shelled and cooked prawns in cocktail sauce. People usually order it for starters.

雞尾酒蝦

雞尾酒蝦是一種裝在玻璃杯的海鮮料理。它包含去殼及煮熟的鮮蝦及雞尾酒醬汁。通常作為前菜食用。

Seafood platter

In general, seafood platter consists of a variety of seafood, such as prawns, crab, salmon, or mackerel. It is a kind of sharing food or starters.

海鮮拼盤

一般而言，海鮮拼盤包含各式各樣的海鮮，像是鮮蝦、蟹、鮭魚、或鯖魚等。它通常為一種分享食物，或者為前菜。

作者給力回答　MP3-30

- copious 豐富度　★★★★★★★★★☆
- creative 創意度　★★★★★★☆☆☆
- impressive 深刻度　★★★★★★★★☆
- vivid 生動程度　★★★★★★★★☆
- pertinent 切題度　★★★★★★☆☆☆

Eating out

　　I want to talk about my favorite restaurant. I went there to celebrate my friend's birthday. We chose this restaurant because it is a well-known French restaurant in the town centre and just fifteen minutes walk from my house. My friend and I had olives and bread, while we were looking at the menu. I chose smoked salmon for a starter, roast duck breast for the main course and crème brûlée for dessert. My friend had French onion soup for the starter, sirloin steak for the main course and chocolate mousse for dessert. I enjoyed the

外出用餐

　　我想要談一間我最喜歡的餐廳。我當時到這間餐廳與朋友慶祝生日。我們當時選這間餐廳的原因是，它是鎮上的一間知名法國餐廳，距離我家也只有十五分鐘路程。我和朋友在看菜單時，先享用了橄欖及法式麵包。我的前菜選了煙燻鮭魚，主菜為法式烤鴨胸，甜點為法式烤布蕾。我的朋友則點了法式洋蔥湯作為前菜，沙朗牛排為主菜，巧克力慕斯為甜點。我特別喜歡烤

暖身話題

休閒話題

生活話題

常考話題

生活話題

roast duck breast the most. Its meat was so tender and juicy. It also went well with the wine we ordered.

Unfortunately, my friend did not like her steak, as she thought it was a bit overcooked. She spoke to a restaurant manager and had a new plate of steak. She was pleased with the second steak they served. We left the restaurant happily after having a three course meal. My friend and I go to this restaurant on a regular basis after we tried its food on her birthday. We both like this restaurant because they serve well-made French dishes with high quality ingredients. I would recommend it to my friends, not just for its food but also as it is good value for money. Most of my friends love the food there.

鴨胸，因它的肉質軟嫩又多汁。搭配我們點的紅酒，口感絕佳。

遺憾地，我的朋友並不喜歡她的牛排，她覺得牛排煎的過熟了。在她和餐廳經理反應後，他們便端上一盤新的牛排。她對於第二盤的牛排感到滿意。我們在享用三道菜後，酒足飯飽的離開。在品嚐過這間餐廳的美食後，我跟朋友就定期的到這間餐廳來用餐。我們倆皆喜歡這間餐廳的原因是，這是採用高品質的食材，精心烹調的法式料理。我會向我其他的朋友們推薦這間餐廳，不僅是它的食物，它也是十分地物超所值。大部分的朋友也愛上這間餐廳的美食。

話題拓展

★ **My favorite restaurant** 最喜歡的餐廳
★ **A well-known French restaurant** 知名法國餐廳
★ **Smoked salmon** 煙燻鮭魚
★ **French onion soup** 法式洋蔥湯
★ **Crème brûlée** 法式烤布蕾
★ **Restaurant manager** 餐廳經理
★ **High quality ingredients** 高品質的食材

Notes

暖身話題

休閒話題

生活話題

常考話題

生活話題

「常考話題」

Baby Daddy — A childhood event

影集內容敘述

　　Ben因先前誤會鄰居Kayla拿了女兒Emma的填充玩具Lamby，而產生了一些不愉快的經驗。當他發現Kayla暗地裡舉辦了幼兒遊戲班，並沒有邀請他和他的女兒Emma後，便憤憤不平地準備重組另一個幼兒遊戲團體，邀請其他鄰居參加。然而，聚會結束後，Ben和家人累壞了，並抱怨鄰居和小孩們多麼的吵鬧。沒想到，其中一位長舌的鄰居還在廁所裡，聽到Ben和家人的對話，並不滿地告訴了其他的鄰居。Ben得知後，因擔心女兒交不到朋友，而借酒澆愁，並在陽台上大叫發洩苦悶。鄰居Kayla聽到了他的對話後，跑上樓想與他爭論，藉由Ben媽媽的勸說，她才打消念頭，並決定邀請他和他的女兒Emma參加幼兒遊戲團體班。

🚗 影集語彙

Out of hand

釋 失去控制

例 The situation is getting a bit out of hand. We need to find a solution to control it.

中 我們必需在情勢變得愈來愈無法控制前處理它。

Toast

釋 敬酒

例 The best man raised his glass in a toast to the bride and groom.

中 伴郎舉杯向新娘及新郎敬酒。

Outcast

釋 被社會拋棄或排斥的人

例 He becomes a social outcast due to a mistake he had made when he was young.

中 年輕時犯的錯誤，使他成為被社會拋棄的人。

Flyer

釋 廣告傳單

例 I received a flyer from a shop. They are doing a half price sale.

中 我收到一間商店的傳單，他們正在做半價的優惠。

Put up with

釋 忍受

例 She can't put up with him anymore and has decided to get a divorce.

中 她無法再容忍他,並決定離婚。

 延伸話題

Role model

A role model is a person who someone admires and serves as a good example to follow.

模範

模範是指令人欽佩的人,及讓大眾仿傚的對象。

Playgroup

A playgroup is an organized group run by parents. The purpose of a playgroup is to let their children play and learn together at regular times in a place outside their homes.

兒童遊戲班

兒童遊戲班為父母所組織的一種團體。它的目的為讓孩子們能互相玩樂及學習。它在固定的時間,並在家以外舉辦。

作者給力回答　　MP3-31

- copious 豐富度　★★★★★★★★★☆
- creative 創意度　★★★★★★☆☆☆
- impressive 深刻度　★★★★★★★★☆☆
- vivid 生動程度　★★★★★★★★★☆
- pertinent 切題度　★★★★★★☆☆☆

A childhood event

I want to talk about my childhood birthday party. My parents held a birthday party for me when I was seven years old. They invited many parents and their children. Most of these parents were from our neighbourhood. Their children were around the same age as me. I had been playing with them since I was five years old.

My parents rented a bouncy castle. All the children were very excited jumping on the bouncy castle. I also played hide-and-seek and

童年事件

我想要談我童年的生日派對。在我七歲時，我的父母為我舉辦了一個生日派對。他們邀請了許多的父母及他們的孩子到派對來。大部分的父母來自於鄰近地區。他們的孩子也與我的年齡相仿。我與這些孩子自五歲起就認識，也一起遊玩。

我的父母租了一個彈力堡，所有的孩子皆興奮地在彈力堡上跳躍。我也與朋友們玩捉迷藏，並共

shared my toys with my friends. While the children were playing, the parents were talking to each other about their jobs, children's schools, and topics related to their children. My mum made some party food for my birthday. Most of it was finger food, such as ham and cheese sandwiches, chicken skewers, hamburgers, cupcakes and fruit, so we could eat and play.

My favourite part of this birthday party was cutting my birthday cake. All my friends sang "Happy Birthday" together before I blew out all the candles on the birthday cake. I received a lot of birthday gifts from my friends and relatives. My favourite gift was a bike. It was helpful because I wanted to ride a cycle to school at that time.

Children who attended the party received party bags before they left. The party bag contained a thank you

享玩具。當孩子們在玩樂時，父母們就聊起工作及孩子的學校等事。我的母親準備了一些派對食物，大部分都是手抓食物，像是火腿起司三明治、雞肉串、漢堡、杯子蛋糕、及水果等。我們才能邊吃邊玩。

我最喜歡的一個部分是切生日蛋糕。所有的朋友在我吹熄蠟燭前，一同為我唱生日快樂歌。我從收到了許多親戚朋友們送的禮物，其中我最喜歡的禮物是一台腳踏車。這非常的實用，因我當時一直想騎車去學校。

參加派對的孩子們在離開時，都收到了一個派對禮物袋。裡頭裝著一個

card and a small toy. The birthday party went very well, my parents liked the hall they hired and also booked it for my brother's birthday.

謝卡，及小玩具。這場生日派對辦得十分成功，我的父們也很喜歡這個場地，並計劃再次訂下這個場地，為我的弟弟舉行生日派對。

💬 話題拓展

★ **Childhood** 童年
★ **Birthday party** 生日派對
★ **Hide-and-seek** 捉迷藏
★ **Party food** 派對食物
★ **Finger food** 手抓食物
★ **A bouncy castle** 彈力堡
★ **Chicken skewers** 雞肉串

Rules of engagement — An unforgettable course

🌲 影集內容敘述

　　Jeff和Audrey夫妻倆經由Adam 和Jennifer的推薦報名了健康飲食烹飪課。課程中，Jeff因受不了Adam的言語刺激，而決定和他一較高下，並請烹飪課老師擔任評審，為倆人的廚藝評分。原本不想加入戰局的Audrey，在Jennifer取笑她的廚藝後，下定決心要贏得比賽。Adam 和Jennifer的廚藝精湛，且賣相佳。相對地，Jeff和Audrey烹飪的食物，不堪入目。意外的是，老師在品嚐Jeff和Audrey的食物後，大讚其餐點口感濃郁，味道鮮美，並宣佈比賽獲勝的是Jeff和Audrey夫妻倆。但是，最後發現Jeff和Audrey違反規則使用牛油及味精，以增添口感，還意外地讓對味精過敏的老師送醫檢查。

影集語彙

Get the hang of something

釋 得知竅門；了解做某事的方法

例 If you keep practicing it, you will get the hang of it.

中 如果你持續練習，你就會了解做這事的方法。

Decipher

釋 辨認；破解

例 Can you decipher the ancient handwriting?

中 你可以辨認古代的手寫字嗎？

Forfeit

釋 因違規而喪失；被沒收

例 This player lost the game by forfeit.

中 這位選手因違規而輸掉比賽。

Troubleshoot

釋 處理難題

例 The system broke down and our supplier has appointed a senior engineer to troubleshoot the problem.

中 系統故障了，我們的供應商指派了一名工程師來處理問題。

Show up

釋 出現；出席

例 I invited Vicky for dinner at seven o'clock but she only

暖身話題

休閒話題

生活話題

常考話題

生活話題

showed up at seven thirty.

中 我邀請Vicky於七點共進晚餐，但她到七點半才出現。

 **延伸話題**

Petty cash

Petty cash is a small amount of money that is kept in the office of a company, for purchasing small items in cash when necessary.

小額現金

Petty cash為辦公室裡的小額現金，主要是用來以現金採買一些小額及必要的物品。

Gratin

Gratin is a dish with a layer of browned crumbs, butter and grated cheese on top. Potato gratin is one of the most common gratin dishes.

奶汁烤菜

Gratin為表面上覆蓋一層麵包屑，奶油，及起司的一道菜。馬鈴薯奶汁烤菜是其中一道最常見的菜餚。

作者給力回答　MP3-32

- copious 豐富度　★★★★★★★★★☆
- creative 創意度　★★★★★★★☆☆☆
- impressive 深刻度　★★★★★★★★☆☆
- vivid 生動程度　★★★★★★★★★☆
- pertinent 切題度　★★★★★★☆☆☆

An unforgettable course

I would like to talk about a course I took at university. This course's name was competitive marketing strategies for global markets. The requirements of this course were to conduct an interview with an international business enterprise and complete a report individually. The topic I chose for this report was an entry strategy to the Chinese market. I had selected a leading international business which had been developing their business in China for over thirty years. I conducted a telephone interview with

難忘的課程

我想要談一個我在大學修的課程。課程名稱是國際市場的行銷競爭策略。這門課程需要訪談一間國際企業，並獨立完成一份報告。我所選擇的主題是進入中國市場的經營策略。我挑選了一間在中國市場發展三十多年的知名的國際企業，並與該公司的行銷經理進行電話訪談。在訪談前，我做了些研究並準備了一系列的問題。作為一個學生，我從課程中學習到許多理論，

203

a marketing manager in that company. Before the interview, I had done a research and prepared a list of questions. As a student, I had learned a lot of theories from the lectures but it is hard to internalize these theories unless you have practical experiences. It was very helpful to gain practical market experience from the marketing manager.

As soon as I collected all the information I needed from the marketing manager, I started to draft my report. It was very difficult for me to understand how the business ran their business in China in the beginning as I did not have relevant work experience. However, I tried to read more relevant literature about how other businesses entered the Chinese market and asked friends who were working in China. Their input helped me to understand their business model.

I worked hard to complete all the

除非你有實際的經驗,理論是很難融會貫通。能從行銷經理取得些實務經驗是非常有助益的。

一旦我從行銷經理那邊收集到我所需要的資訊,我便開始撰寫報告。剛開始時,因為我沒有相關的經驗,挺難領會他們在中國的經營模式。然而,我試著閱讀一些關於其他企業如何進入中國市場的相關文獻,以及詢問在中國工作的朋友。這也幫助我了解他們的經營模式。

我十分努力地完成這

requirements of the report and submitted it on time. The lecturer was very satisfied with my report and I gained very good marks in this subject.

份報告所需的條件，並準時提交報告。該課程講師十分滿意我的報告內容，並給了我高分。

💬 話題拓展

★ **Entry strategy** 進入策略
★ **An international business enterprise** 知名的國際企業
★ **Telephone interview** 電話訪談
★ **Marketing manager** 行銷經理
★ **Literature** 文獻
★ **Lecturer** 講師
★ **Requirements of the report** 這份報告所需的條件

Neighbors — Something Did not Go as Planned

🌿 影集內容敘述

　　Amy向Sheldon提議搭乘Vintage火車到Napa Valley一起共渡情人節週末，並邀請了朋友Bernadette和Howard一同共遊。熱愛火車的Sheldon一搭上火車後，就興奮地四處探望。當他們在火車上享用晚餐時，Sheldon認識了一位也是火車愛好者的乘客Eric，倆人一拍即合，高談闊論彼此搭乘火車的經驗，獨留Amy坐在餐桌。Bernadette因不願Amy被冷落，而提醒Sheldon這是他們的情人節晚餐，他應該陪伴其女友。然而，遲鈍的Sheldon竟邀請Eric回他們的餐桌，再續火車的話題。在Eric及Sheldon去參觀車掌室回來後，Amy忍無可忍，便請Eric暫時離開，並向Sheldon抱怨今晚本應是浪漫的情人節夜晚，但她卻坐了一個晚上的冷板凳。

影集語彙

For a laugh

釋 開玩笑

例 Just for a laugh. Don't be too serious.

中 只是開個玩笑，別太認真。

For starters

釋 首先

例 A: Why did you decide not to go to university? B: For starters, tuition fees for universities are very expensive. Not everyone can afford it now.

中 A：為何你決定不繼續升大學？B：首先，現在大學學費十分高昂，不是每個人都付擔的起。

Magnificent

釋 極好的；壯麗的；極美的

例 This is the best national park I have ever been to. It has magnificent views.

中 這是我去過最好的國家公園，它的景色極為壯麗。

Entrée

釋 【英國用法】在主菜前的小菜；【美國用法】主菜

例 You can choose an entrée of salmon, chicken or duck.

中 您在主菜前的小菜可選擇鮭魚、雞肉、或鴨肉。

Fixer-upper

釋 需要整修的舊房子

例 He bought a fixer-upper at an auction, made the repairs and resold later at a profit.

中 他在拍賣會上買了一間需整修的舊房子，重新裝修，再賣掉賺價差。

 延伸話題

Bed and breakfast

Bed and breakfast is also called "B & B". It offers an overnight accommodation and breakfast. In general, bed and breakfast are in family homes with less than ten bedrooms.

住宿及早餐

住宿及早餐又稱 "B & B"。它提供過夜住宿及早餐。一般而言，住宿及早餐位於少於十間房間的家庭式房屋。

Risotto

Risotto is a North Italian dish of rice with ingredients such as broth, mushroom, vegetables, meat, seafood, wine or butter.

義式燉飯

義式燉飯為北義大利的一種米料理。原料像是高湯、蘑菇、蔬菜、肉、海鮮、酒、或奶油等。

MP3-33

作者給力回答

- copious 豐富度　★★★★★★★★★☆
- creative 創意度　★★★★★★★☆☆☆
- impressive 深刻度　★★★★★★★★☆☆
- vivid 生動程度　★★★★★★★★★☆
- pertinent 切題度　★★★★★★★☆☆☆

Describe a trip did not go as planned

When I flew from Taipei to London a few years ago, there was an engine problem in the aircraft I planned to board. All the passengers had to wait at the airport for six hours. The long wait was tedious and tiring. Due to the late departure, I missed a connecting flight from Amsterdam to London. When I arrived in Amsterdam, it was ten o'clock in the evening. I was exhausted and hungry. Luckily, the airline company provided overnight accommodation and meals. I stayed

未如預定計劃的旅行

幾年前，當我從台北飛往倫敦時，我欲搭乘的飛機引擎故障。所有的旅客在機場等候超過六個小時。這漫長的等待十分地冗長及疲累。由於飛機晚起飛的關係，我錯過了飛往阿姆斯特丹到倫敦的轉接班機。當我抵達阿姆斯特丹時，已經是晚上十點了。我當時又餓又累。幸好航空公司有提供過境旅館及餐點。我在機場附近的旅館住了一夜後，便搭

暖身話題

休閒話題

生活話題

常考話題

生活話題

in a hotel near the airport for a night and got the next day's early flight to London.

Since the ground staff at the airport were very helpful and the hotel room was comfortable, it made me feel better after the long wait at Taipei airport. Luckily, I didn't have to go to work next day because I had one day to adjust to the time difference. On the other hand, some passengers were not happy because they had to go back to work the next day and would probably lose a day's pay. Although waiting at the airport for so long was not pleasant, I think it is very important to make sure that aircraft are safe. I will still travel with this airline because they were able to deal with a contingency and were willing to reimburse passengers for any costs relevant to the delay.

乘隔天早上的班機回倫敦。

由於機場地勤人員皆十分地友善，且旅館房間很舒適的關係，即使在漫長的等待後，也覺得沒這麼槽。幸運的是，我隔天不需要回公司上班，因為我特別保留了一天，以調整時差。另一方面，有些旅客就不怎麼開心，因他們隔天還要上班，並可能因延誤而損失一天的工資。雖然在機場等待並不愉悅，但確保飛機能安全起飛是非常重要的。我將來還是會搭乘這家航空公司，因為他們能處理緊急事件，及願意賠償旅客因延誤所造成的損失。

💬 話題拓展

★ **Engine failure** 引擎故障
★ **Passengers** 旅客
★ **Overnight accommodation** 過夜旅館
★ **Ground staff** 地勤人員
★ **Airline** 航空公司
★ **Contingency** 緊急事件
★ **Reimburse passengers** 賠償旅客

Notes

Rules of Engagement — Describe a charitable work

🌲 影集內容敘述

　　Jeff的辦公室興起了一股捐款的熱潮，舉凡合買彩券、集資合買同事的生日蛋糕、捐助公益活動等。一向對於捐款極排斥的Jeff，斬釘截鐵地對其同事表示，他不會參與任何捐款性質的活動。然而，他這回踢到鐵板了，他的太太Audrey正計劃籌備一個慈善路跑的活動，需要Jeff遊說其同事集資捐款。Jeff實在拉不下臉來說服他的同事，本想自己掏腰包解決這件事，但他得知若Audrey跑完全程10KM，就必需捐一千五百元美金。為避免捐助這筆錢，他想到的唯一辦法即是阻止Audrey參加路跑活動。他在Audrey的飲料中下安眠藥，使她睡過頭，無法參加路跑。Jeff以為事情到這就告一段落，沒想到，Audrey為彌補自己睡過頭的錯誤，決定自行掏腰包捐一千五百元美金。

🚗 影集語彙

Outfit

釋 為特定場合穿的全套服裝

例 I bought this outfit for the fancy dress party.

中 我為了化裝舞會買了這套服裝。

Hang out with

釋 經常到某處或與某人廝混

例 The police found out where the suspects hung out.

中 警察發現嫌疑犯都在哪些地方廝混。

Stress somebody out

釋 使某人緊張

例 Job appraisals stressed her out.

中 工作評估令她非常地緊張。

Take something to the next level

釋 帶領某物到下一個階段

例 Three years of taking charge of the Marketing Department, Joey is ready to take it to the next level.

中 在掌管行銷部門三年，Joey準備好帶領該部門到下一個階段。

Obstacle

釋 障礙

> **例** There are many obstacles for him to overcome.
>
> **中** 他的一生中有許多障礙要克服。

 **延伸話題**

Charity run

A charity run is an uncompetitive race and usually being held to raise money for the charity.

公益路跑

Charity run為一種非競賽性的路跑，通常為慈善機構募款所發起。

Baby Shower

A baby shower is a party to celebrate a pending or recent child birth. Guests usually bring baby related gifts to the expectant mother or parents.

寶寶派對

Baby Shower為慶祝寶寶出生或在寶寶出生前所舉辦的一個派對。參加的賓客們通常會送寶寶相關禮物給準媽媽或父母。

作者給力回答　MP3-34

- copious 豐富度　★★★★★★★★☆
- creative 創意度　★★★★★★☆☆☆
- impressive 深刻度　★★★★★★★☆☆
- vivid 生動程度　★★★★★★★★☆
- pertinent 切題度　★★★★★★☆☆☆

Describe a charitable work

I would like to talk about a charity run organised by my colleague Louise. After her mother suffered from the misery of breast cancer and died two years ago, she raised funds for breast cancer research by organizing a charity run. She asked her friends and colleagues for donations. When the fund reached £10,000, she ran a marathon.

Her friends and colleagues thought her charitable work was very significant because her mother died from breast cancer and she wanted to

慈善活動

我想要談一個由我同事Louise所舉辦的慈善路跑。由於她的母親深受乳癌之苦並於兩年前過世，她想要藉由慈善路跑來募款，以幫助乳癌研究及那些患有乳癌的病人。她請朋友及同事們捐款。若她籌到10,000英鎊，她將在市區進行馬拉松賽跑。

她的朋友及同事們覺得這個公益活動深具意義。由於她的母親死於乳癌，她想為那些受相同病

do something for people who suffer from similar illnesses. She accumulated the fund quickly and reached £10,000 within two weeks. She did her marathon in the city and then donated all the money she raised to a breast cancer charitable foundation.

Fundraising is very common in the UK. You can raise funds for charity or for individual purposes. If your friend suffers from a rare disease, you can organise an event to raise money for your friend's medical expenses. Online fundraising has become prevalent recently. You can send an online fundraising link to your friends or add it to your Facebook. All the donations will be made online. If you reach your fundraising goal, you can withdraw the money, and donate the money. Since the majority of British people are willing to help with charitable works and generous, fundraising is popular in the UK.

苦的人們盡一點棉薄之力。她很快地在兩週內籌到10,000英鎊。她完成馬拉松賽跑，並將募款捐給乳癌研究基金會。

募款在英國非常地普遍。你可以為慈善募款或個人募款。假如你的朋友得了罕見疾病，你可以規劃一個活動來幫助你的朋友籌措醫療費用。近年來，網路募款也漸漸盛行。你可以寄一個網路募款連結給你的朋友，或將它加到你的Facebook。所有的捐款在網路上進行。假使你達到了募款目標，你可以再取得募款金額。由於大部分的英國人皆樂意幫忙慈善活動且慷慨，募款在英國很盛行。

話題拓展

★ **A charity run** 慈善路跑
★ **Colleague** 同事
★ **Marathon** 馬拉松
★ **Suffer from** 受…之苦
★ **Donation** 捐款
★ **Fundraising** 籌款
★ **Rare disease** 罕見疾病
★ **Job opening** 徵才

Notes

My family — Describe a challenge you had in your life

🌿 影集內容敘述

　　Susan被選為同學會的發言人，正當她滿心歡喜地準備發言稿，一個突如其來的打擊，令原本充滿自信的她一蹶不振。Susan的公司正在進行縮編，考量縮減她的工時，並找了一位年輕的員工來取代她。Susan受不了這種屈辱，當下就自願請辭。她在這個打擊下，幾日來愁眉不展，鬱鬱寡歡。在家人及朋友的鼓勵下，Susan才重拾信心，振作起來。正當她準備去參加同學會的前一刻，她接到前公司的來電，原本繼任她的員工不適任，前公司希望Susan能重回工作崗位。在聽到這個好消息後，Susan開心且充滿自信的去參加同學會。

🚗 影集語彙

Thrive on something
- 釋 在壓力或困境中仍樂在其中
- 例 Although this job is stressful, I thrive on it.
- 中 雖然這份工作壓力很大，我仍樂在其中。

Show someone the ropes
- 釋 教（某人）如何工作
- 例 Susan does not want to show her replacement the ropes.
- 中 Susan並不想要教接替她的人做她的工作。

Onwards and upwards
- 釋 愈來愈成功
- 例 My favourite football team is moving onwards and upwards.
- 中 我最喜歡的足球隊表現愈來愈好。

Put all eggs in one basket
- 釋 把所有的雞蛋放在同一個籃子裡
- 例 You should diversify your investment plan. Do not put all your eggs in one basket.
- 中 你應該分散投資風險，不要把所有的雞蛋放在同一個籃子裡。

Heartwarming
- 釋 感人的

> **例** This is a heartwarming story of a family reunion.
> **中** 這是一個感人的家人團圓故事。

延伸話題

Event organizer

An event organizer's job involves a wide range of activities for event creations, such as liaising with clients and suppliers for event requirements, organizing the venue, caterers, contractors, equipment hire, and so on.

活動籌備者

Event organizer的工作包含許多與活動籌備相關的任務，像是與客戶與供應商洽談活動規劃細節，統籌場地、餐飲、承包商、器材租借等事宜。

Cutback

A cutback usually means a reduction of spending or the number of workers in a company in order to save money.

削減

Cutback通常指公司為省錢而進行的削減，如削減花費，或削減人力等。

作者給力回答　🎙 MP3-35

- copious 豐富度　★★★★★★★★★☆
- creative 創意度　★★★★★★☆☆☆
- impressive 深刻度　★★★★★★★★☆
- vivid 生動程度　★★★★★★★★☆
- pertinent 切題度　★★★★★★★☆☆☆

Describe a challenge you had in your life

I have had many challenges in my life, such as studying and working abroad. I don't really mind taking challenges, as long as they are positive ones. One of the challenges I had in my life was to find my first job in the UK. Since applicants in the UK need to have UK work experience to find a job, finding a first job in the UK is tough for people who have no work experience.

Although I had a few years work experience in my country, most British companies don't really

人生的挑戰

我的人生中有許多的挑戰，像是出國留學及工作。只要是正面的挑戰，我並不會排斥這些挑戰。我人生中的一個挑戰為在英國找我的第一份工作。找第一份工作對於在英國無工作經驗的人十分地困難，因為大部分的工作皆要求應徵者具有英國的工作經驗。

雖然我在我的國家有幾年的工作經驗，大部分的英國公司不認可海外的

recognise overseas work experience. I had to start over.

After sending countless job applications and attending many interviews, I eventually got my first job in the UK. I passed two paper tests and two interviews to get this job. I was pleased because this was a job I really wanted. There were many obstacles during my job-hunt, but because of my perseverance, I got my dream job.

I spoke to my manager after I joined the company. Apparently, my manager was looking for a candidate with international marketing experience. However, candidates he had interviewed with did not meet this requirement. I was the only one who met the requirement. In addition, my company did not have job openings for a long time. I felt I was very lucky to find the right job at the right time.

工作經驗，我必須從頭來過。

在寄了無數份的工作申請，及參加過許多的面試後，我最終找到了我在英國的第一份工作。我通過了兩次筆試及兩次面試才找到這份工作。我當時非常地開心，因這是我想要的工作。在求職過程中，遇到許多的障礙。但我的毅力，我找到我的夢想工作。

在加入公司後，與我的上司談過。實際上，我的上司當時在找一個具有國際行銷企劃經驗的人。然而，他面試的候選人都不具此資格。我是唯一具有此條件的候選人。此外，我的公司已很久沒有徵才。我當時覺得自已很幸運能在對的時機找到對的工作。

話題拓展

★ **Challenge** 挑戰
★ **Countless** 無數的
★ **Job-hunting** 求職
★ **Perseverance** 堅持不懈
★ **Interviews** 面試
★ **Job opening** 徵才
★ **The only one who met the requirement** 唯一具有此條件的候選人

Notes

My family — Describe an event you attended

🌿 影集內容敘述

　　Susan和Janey參加一位朋友的單身告別派對。沒想到，當朋友Kirsty抵達派對時，竟然表示未婚夫在最後一刻拋棄了她，明天的婚禮舉行不成了。看著傷心欲絕的Kirsty，Susan決定幫她聯絡其未婚夫，好讓他回心轉意。然而，她的未婚夫到場後，表示他臨陣脫逃的原因是他認為他可以找到更好的伴侶。Susan氣急敗壞的向Kirsty表示，離開他才是最好的選擇。若她真的嫁給他，才是人生中的最大敗筆。

影集語彙

There are plenty more fish in the sea

釋 這個不成，好的人還很多

說 當某人的一段感情結束時，可用此句安慰來表示好的人還很多。

例 There are plenty more fish in the sea. The next one might be better.

中 這個不成，好的人還很多。下個人選也許更好。

An ace up one's sleeve

釋 秘密王牌

說 指暗中保留的計劃或事物，等待有利時機時，發揮它的作用。

例 I guess Jack still has an ace up his sleeve. We just don't know about it.

中 我猜Jack一定還有一個秘密王牌。我們只是不知道而已。

Waste of space

釋 無用之人；無用之物

例 He is fifty years old and still sponges off his parents. He is such a waste of space.

中 他都已經五十歲了，還靠父母養他。真是無用之人。

In a nutshell

釋 簡短說明

例 Since the CEO hasn't got a lot of time to go through all the details, please put it in a nutshell.

中 總經理的時間有限，請簡短說明。

Brag about

釋 吹噓；自誇

例 She likes bragging about how rich she is.

中 她喜歡向人吹噓她的財富。

 延伸話題

A hen night

A hen party is a party held for the bride-to-be before her wedding. In general, the bride-to-be's friends organise the party and select entertainments which best pleases the bride-to-be. Friends usually give advice to the bride-to-be before her wedding date. The term hen party is commonly used in the United Kingdom, and the term bachelorette party is commonly used in the United States.

女性婚前的派對

Hen party是專門為準新娘於婚禮前所舉辦的派對。一般而言，準新娘的朋友們會籌備派對，並選擇適合準新娘的娛樂活動。朋友們通常也會在這天給她一些婚前建議。Hen party為英國的用法，在美國則稱為bachelorette party。

Amateur

An amateur is a person who is engaged in an art, sport, or science activity for pleasure, not as a job.

業餘從事者

Amateur為從事藝術、運動、或科學領域的業餘從事者。他們通常將其愛好的活動做為消遣娛樂，而非正式的工作。

 作者給力回答　　MP3-36

- copious 豐富度　★★★★★★★★★☆
- creative 創意度　★★★★★★☆☆☆
- impressive 深刻度　★★★★★★★★☆☆
- vivid 生動程度　★★★★★★★★★☆
- pertinent 切題度　★★★★★★☆☆☆

Describe an event you attended

I would like to talk about a hen party I attended. My friends and I tried to organise a hen night for a bride-to-be a few years ago. My friends and I had been thinking what would best please the bride-to-be. We

參加過的活動

我想要談我參加過的一個女性婚前派對。幾年前，我和朋友們為一名即將結婚的女性朋友規劃了一個婚前派對。我和朋友們一直在想如何打造一個

decided to have a spa treatment in a luxury hotel because the bride-to-be told us that she just wanted to have a relaxing weekend.

We chose a hotel in the countryside with a lakeside view and spa facilities. Its facilities include a swimming pool, a steam room, and a sauna. There were a range of treatments, such as skin facials and deep muscle massage. They also had beauty therapists to do nails and tanning. It was a great place to spoil her on her hen night.

We arrived at the hotel in the evening and had a delicious meal at the hotel. After the meal, we had a few drinks at the bar and gave our advice to the bride-to-be before her big day. We enjoyed the spa treatments next day and walked around the lake. We had lunch at the hotel and went home in the afternoon.

令她開心的派對。由於這名準新娘曾告訴我們,她想要有一個悠閒的週末,所以我們最後決定帶她一間豪華的飯店享受SPA。

我們選了一間位於郊外,附有湖景及SPA設施的飯店。它的設施包含了游泳池、蒸氣室、桑拿浴。它有一系列的美容服務,像是臉部保養、深層按摩。它們還有美容師來做美甲、人工日光浴的服務。這是個讓她在婚前派對上恣意享受的好地方。

我們在傍晚抵達飯店,並於飯店內享用美味的晚餐。在餐後,我們一同聚集在酒吧飲酒,並給她一些婚前建議。隔天,我們便一起享受SPA,在沿著湖邊散步。在飯店內用過午餐後,我們於下午啟程回家。這真是個奢華

It was truly a paradise of luxury and indulgence. The bride-to-be was very happy about the hotel we chose and enjoyed all the activities we organised. Since the hen night went very well, some of our friends wanted to have their hen weekends at this hotel before they got married.

和享受的天堂。準新娘十分滿意我們所選的飯店及規劃的活動。由於這個女性婚前派對辦的很成功，一些朋友們也想在這間飯店舉辦她們的女性婚前派對週末。

💬 話題拓展

★ **Bride-to-be** 準新娘
★ **Steam room** 蒸氣室
★ **A swimming pool** 游泳池
★ **A steam room** 蒸氣室
★ **Sauna** 桑拿浴
★ **Skin facial** 臉部保養
★ **Tanning** 人工日光浴

暖身話題

休閒話題

生活話題

常考話題

生活話題

Friends — Describe a letter

🌲 影集內容敘述

　　Monica和Chandler準備要領養一個孩子。他們需要找一位推薦人幫他們寫推薦信，以向領養中心證實他們將會是合適的父母。Monica和Chandler起初找了好友Rachel來幫忙，但Joey表示他認識Chandler多年，更能勝任這個工作。Joey求好心切，想用更好的文字來修飾他的句子。他便使用電腦同義字功能，找出其他的替代字。沒想到，他將整封信修飾的詞不達意。Monica和Chandler看過信後，希望Joey能以發自內心的方式來撰寫這封信。Joey最後決定手寫這封信，並直接寄給領養中心。Monica和Chandler夫妻倆發現他未經他們確認就直接把信寄出後，驚慌失措地打電話給領養中心。但領養中心誤以為這封信為小孩所撰寫，並表示喜歡這種新奇的方式，也接受他們的申請。

影集語彙

Sharp as a tack

釋 聰明的；有才智的

例 Michelle is as sharp as a tack. She can do this job very well.

中 Michelle十分聰明伶俐，必定能勝任這個工作。

Oversight

釋 疏忽出錯

例 This mistake was due to an oversight. They have made the correction.

中 這個錯誤是因疏忽而起。他們已經更正這個錯誤了。

Tacky

釋 品質低劣的；俗氣的

例 This outfit looks tacky. If I were you, I wouldn't wear this outfit in this occasion.

中 這套服裝很俗氣。假如我是你，我不會在這種場合穿這套衣服。

Self-centred

釋 自我中心的；自私自利的

例 He is so self-centred and wouldn't help us when we were in trouble.

中 他十分的自私自利，即便我們有難時，他也不願伸出援手。

暖身話題

休閒話題

生活話題

常考話題

生活話題

Flip out

釋 大發雷霆

例 She will flip out if you hurt her child.

中 如果你傷害她的小孩的話，她會大發雷霆。

 **延伸話題**

Letters of recommendation

There are different types of letter of recommendations, such as letters for a university application, a job application or a personal letter. The academic reference letters are usually written by professors or supervisors. The employment recommendation letters are usually written by managers or bosses.

推薦信

推薦信有許多種類，如大學申請的推薦信、工作申請的推薦信、或個人推薦信。學術性的推薦信通常為教授或指導老師所撰寫。而求職推薦信則由上司或老闆撰寫。

Thesaurus

Thesaurus is a dictionary which provides words with similar meanings. The benefit of using a thesaurus is to look up a similar word which could help you express well.

同義詞詞典

Thesaurus為提供同義詞的詞典。此字典的好處為可查詢類似意思的字，以利表達。

作者給力回答 MP3-37

- **copious** 豐富度　★★★★★★★★★☆
- **creative** 創意度　★★★★★★☆☆☆
- **impressive** 深刻度　★★★★★★★★☆
- **vivid** 生動程度　★★★★★★★★★☆
- **pertinent** 切題度　★★★★★★☆☆☆

Describe a letter

I would like to talk about a letter I received from my father. When I was eleven years old, my father wrote me a letter. Since most people use e-mails, text messages, or social media networks to communicate with each other nowadays, it was very unusual to receive a handwritten letter.

He thought it was a good way to

描述一封信

　　我想要談一封我父親寫給我的信。當我十一歲時，我的父親寫了封信給我。由於現今大部分的人都用電子郵件、簡訊、或社交網絡來溝通，收到手寫信是十分地罕見。

　　他認為這是比直接對

暖身話題

休閒話題

生活話題

常考話題

生活話題

communicate with me, rather than talking to me directly. As I was about to enter my teenage years, he wanted to let me know how to become a young lady and how to talk to people. I was only a child and felt he was very old-school parent and I wasn't paying attention to what he said at that time. However, I kept this letter and read it after I became an adult. I felt this letter was so meaningful. It showed how a father cared about his daughter. He probably didn't know how to talk to me face to face, so he put all his thoughts in a letter and gave it to me.

I actually think letters are an effective way to express yourself because you might misinterpret other communication. If you have physical letters, you can keep them forever and read them when you are older. I guess this is why most people still give physical birthday cards nowadays, because they are

話還好的溝通方法。由於我當時正值轉變為青少年，他想要讓我知道如何成為一位淑女，及一些待人處世的道理。我當時還只是一個孩子，覺得他很老派，並沒有注意他所說的話。然而，當我成年再讀起這封信時，我覺得這封信意義深長。它表現了一位父親如何關心他的女兒。他可能與我面對面時，不知道說什麼，所以將他想表達的想法化為文字寫給我。

我覺得這是一個十分有效益的溝通模式，因為或許在言語的詮釋上會有些誤解。若你有實體信件，你可以將它永久保留，並於年長後再讀。我猜這也是為何大多數的人還給實體生日卡片的原因，因這樣比較周到。我

thoughtful. I really appreciate what my father did. I still enjoy reading his letter during different stages of my life.

很感謝我的父親為我所做的一切，我還是很喜歡在我人生的不同階段，閱讀他所寫給我的信。

💬 話題拓展

★ **A handwritten letter** 手寫信
★ **E-mails** 電子郵件
★ **Social media** 社交網絡
★ **Old-school** 老派的
★ **Misinterpret** 誤解
★ **Thoughtful** 考量周到的
★ **Physical letters** 實體信件

Friends — Describe a game show you love

🌲 影集內容敘述

　　Joey受邀參加美國當紅的益智節目Pyramid。參賽隊伍為兩組，每組兩人。競賽的規則為每隊參賽者互相猜出對方所形容的事物，猜對者即得分。Joey在第一、二回合表現不佳，且其滑稽的作答方式，惹惱了參賽同伴。第三回合為他主導形容美國國會的專有名詞，讓參賽同伴進行搶答。然而，Joey對美國國會的專有名詞一概不知，只能淪落所有問題都"跳過"的窘境。原本想可能會一路慘到底的Joey，竟然在最後回合捲土重來，反敗為勝，令人跌破眼鏡。

影集語彙

Pass the torch (to somebody)

釋　傳授

例　Derek become too old to run his bakery, so he passed the torch to his oldest son.

中　Derek年事已高，所以將餅店生意傳授給他的大兒子。

Jeopardize

釋　危及，損害

例　If you don't complete this project, it might jeopardize your chances of next project.

中　假如你不完成這個專案，可能會危及你接下一個案子。

Eye candy

釋　華而不實

例　Those images on the website are just eye candy. I don't think we can attract long-term customers.

中　在網站上的圖片，雖然吸引人，卻無內涵。我不覺得我們會藉此吸引永久客戶。

Contestant

釋　參賽選手

例　Some actresses are former contestants of beauty pageants.

中　一些女演員曾參加過選美比賽。

Alumni

釋 校友

例 Howard has been selected as the head of alumni association.

中 Howard被選為校友會的會長。

延伸話題

A game show

A game show is a type of television programme where contestants play games and answer questions in order to win prizes.

電視遊戲節目

Game show為一種電視遊戲節目。它的形式為參賽者玩遊戲，及回答問題，以贏得獎品。

Nursery rhymes

A nursery rhyme is a short and simple song for children, such as Twinkle, Twinkle, Little Star, old MacDonald had a farm and so on.

兒歌

Nursery rhymes為一種專門為兒童設計的簡易歌曲。例如，小星星、王老先生等歌曲。

作者給力回答　MP3-38

- copious 豐富度　★★★★★★★★★☆
- creative 創意度　★★★★★★☆☆☆
- impressive 深刻度　★★★★★★★★☆☆
- vivid 生動程度　★★★★★★★★☆
- pertinent 切題度　★★★★★★☆☆☆

Describe a game show you love

My favourite game show is a British TV programme. Unlike a traditional game show, this TV programme features a large coin pusher arcade-style machine. The TV presenter asks contestants a range of questions, such as history, films, food, festivals and so on. If the contestants answer correctly, they earn tokens to drop into the coin pusher machine. There are four drop zones in the machine. Contestants can select a drop zone which is more likely to push some of the other coins

喜愛的益智節目

我最喜歡的一個益智節目為一個英國的節目。不同於傳統的益智節目，這個節目的特色為一台大型的遊樂場推幣機。節目主持人會問參賽者一系列的問題，像是歷史、電影、美食、節慶等。假如參賽者答對了，他們將贏得籌碼，並可投入推幣機內。推幣機內有四個投入區。參賽者可選擇他們認為最有可能將硬幣推出的一個投入區。假使硬幣落

off the edge. If coins move to the win zone, they get prizes. Coins are worth £50 each. The player who accumulates the most amount of money will have a chance to play for the jackpot of ten thousand pounds.

One of the most memorable episodes I watched was about a contestant who won the jackpot of £10,000. He told the presenter that he wanted to win the prize because his daughter was going to get married, so extra money would help him to organise the wedding. He answered most questions correctly and used a winning tactic to play the machine. His tactic was to stay in the same drop zone and drop the tokens in good time. Apart from general knowledge, contestants have to use their tactics to win the game.

I like this TV programme because I love playing the coin pusher machine and I can also learn

入獎區，參賽者即可獲得獎金。每個硬幣值50英鎊。而累積最多獎金的玩家將有機會獲得10,000英鎊的頭獎。

其中我印象最深的一集是關於一位贏得頭獎10,000英鎊的參賽者。他告訴主持人他想要得獎的目的是他的女兒即將於今年結婚，獎金可幫助他籌備女兒的婚禮。他答對了大部分的問題，並善用策略來玩推幣機。他的策略為專攻一個投入區，及選對時機投入硬幣。除了一般的答題知識外，參賽者還要懂得運用策略來贏得這場比賽。

我喜歡這個電視節目的原因為我平時喜歡玩推幣機，並且也可從節目中

some knowledge from watching the show.

學習一些知識。

話題拓展

★ **A coin pusher** 遊樂場的推幣機
★ **Arcade** 遊樂場
★ **Festival** 節慶
★ **Contestant** 參賽者
★ **Tactic** 策略
★ **Jackpot** 頭彩
★ **The most memorable episodes** 最令人印象深刻的集數

暖身話題

休閒話題

生活話題

常考話題

生活話題

Melissa & Joey — Describe a friend

🍃 影集內容敘述

　　Melissa和Joey認識了一對新婚不久的夫婦 – Nate 和 Gillian。Melissa一直想與其他對的夫婦做朋友，因此十分重視這段友誼。Joey 與Nate某次在健身房聊天時，Nate提及他對Gillian的感情已漸行漸遠，並有意分手。Joey聽到後十分震驚，並承諾會幫Nate保守秘密。回到家後，Melissa發覺Joey有事隱瞞，並逼供他說出這個秘密。Joey逼不得已將Nate的秘密說出來，但希望Melissa能保密。Melissa雖口頭答應，但卻在一次與Gillian的聚會上，脫口說出這件事。Nate在發現Melissa和Joey洩露秘密後，大為光火，並拒絕出席原本約好的聚餐以示抗議。他並請服務生轉交他的親筆信給Melissa和Joey，表達他的不滿，並在信中透露Melissa和Joey曾跟他夫妻倆講彼此壞話的內容，以示報復。但Melissa和Joey為了表示信任對方而拒絕再閱讀信件。

🚗 影集語彙

Well-meaning

(釋) 善意的，但卻事與願違

(例) I know Jeff is well-meaning, but I wish he wouldn't interfere.

(中) 我知道Jeff是出於善意，但我希望他不要插手此事。

Chit-chat

(釋) 閒談

(例) What did Judy and Robin talk about? Just chit-chat.

(中) Judy和Robin在談論什麼？只是閒聊而已。

Spill the beans

(釋) 洩漏秘密

(例) She is disappointed because her best friend spilt the beans.

(中) 她很失望，因為她最好的朋友洩漏了她的秘密。

Boot somebody out of something

(釋) 把某人趕出去

(例) He was booted out of his school due to his absence from school.

(中) 因為他曠課，而被學校趕了出去。

Manipulation

(釋) 操縱

> **例** This company has been accused of media manipulation.
>
> **中** 這間公司被指控操縱媒體。

🎈 延伸話題

Pompeii

Pompeii is an ancient Roman city near the Bay of Naples in Italy. Pompeii was destroyed during an eruption of Mount Vesuvius in 79 A.D. The objects underneath the dust and debris had been preserved for centuries. The remaining buildings have shown us everyday life in an ancient Roman city.

龐貝

龐貝為義大利那不勒斯灣附近的一座古羅馬城市。在公元79年，龐貝遭受到維蘇威火山爆發而被摧毀。在火山灰及殘骸下的物品皆被保存了幾個世紀。保留下來的建築物呈現了古羅馬時期人民的日常生活。

Vault

A vault is a secure room in a bank with think walls and strong doors. People keep valuables, money and documents in the vaults.

金庫

Vault 是指位於銀行內含有堅固厚牆門的房間。人們通常在金庫裡保存貴重物品、金錢、及文件。

 作者給力回答　　MP3-39

- copious 豐富度　★★★★★★★★★☆
- creative 創意度　★★★★★★☆☆☆
- impressive 深刻度　★★★★★★★★☆☆
- vivid 生動程度　★★★★★★★★★☆
- pertinent 切題度　★★★★★★★☆☆☆

暖身話題

休閒話題

生活話題

常考話題

生活話題

Describe a friend

　　I would like to talk about my friend - Sharon. I met her when I studied business school at college. Although we grew up in different backgrounds and lived in different cities, our friendship developed quickly after we met. She was a kind and warm-hearted person. She likes helping people and making friends. Whenever I was depressed, she listened to me and gave me advice. I enjoy spending time with her because we both like reading and travelling. I had many pleasant memories with her when I was in the university.

描述一位朋友

　　我想要談我的朋友 Sharon。她是在我上大學讀商學院時認識的。雖然我們成長於不同的背景及居住在不同的城市，我們一見如故，很快地就成為朋友。她是一位善良且熱心腸的人。她喜歡幫助人，並廣結善緣。每當我沮喪時，她聽我訴苦並給我建議。我喜歡與她相處，因我們都喜愛閱讀及旅行。我跟她擁有許多大學時期的美好回憶。

She is also a smart and talented lady. She was one of few students whose dissertations were awarded distinctions by the school. I was so proud of her when I heard the news. She has considerable business acumen. While the majority of my classmates were looking for their first jobs, she had already started a business. She knew what business she wanted to do and what target customers she wanted to get. Her business went very well and she expanded business operations.

Due to my job relocation, we live in different countries now. We don't really see each other often, but we still keep in touch by e-mail or telephone. When I have a holiday, I always try my best to visit her. I think a good friendship is difficult to find, I feel lucky to have met such a nice person at college.

她十分地聰穎及具有天份。她是在大學裡少數論文獲得優等的學生。當我聽到這個好消息時，我以她為榮。她在生意上相當的精明。當大部分的同學還在找第一份工作時，她已經開始做生意。她清楚她想要做的生意及目標客群。她的生意經營的很好，並且拓展了營運。

由於我的工作調動的關係，我們目前居住在不同的國家。我們並不常見面，但還是常用電子郵件及電話聯繫。每當我有假期時，我總是去拜訪她。一段好的友情很難得，我很幸運能在大學裡認識她。

💬 話題拓展

★ **Business school** 商學院
★ **Reading** 閱讀
★ **Travelling** 旅行
★ **Distinction** 優等
★ **Acumen** 精明
★ **Target customers** 目標客群
★ **Relocation** 改變地點
★ **Different countries** 不同的國家

Notes

Melissa & Joey — A second language you want to learn (except English)

🌿 影集內容敘述

　　Melissa想邀請一間日本企業到美國投資並設立據點，並想請諳日語的Joey教她幾句實用日語，以讓對方留下好印象。然而，在聚會當天，Melissa發現日本客戶一句英語也不會，只好立即請Joey到現場協助翻譯。Joey很盡力地翻譯，並與客戶打好關係。然而，他發現這名客戶對Melissa感興趣，並邀Melissa一起回飯店飲酒。Joey為了要保護她，就故意說Melissa腹瀉，需回家休息。隔天，Melissa收到來自於日本客戶的一束花，及一張卡片。卡片寫著希望她腹瀉的狀況能好轉。Melissa得知後，十分地氣Joey沒照實際情況翻譯，並再接受日本客戶的邀請，赴飯店找他。到了飯店後，Melissa才發現他的房間裡，另有一名招待女郎，Melissa發覺情況不對，便找藉口離開了。這時她才了解Joey當時是想保護她。

🚗 影集語彙

Woo

- 釋 努力說服；爭取
- 例 The opposition party is trying to woo the voters before the election.
- 中 在野黨在選舉前，極力爭取選民的支持。

Fizzle out

- 釋 虎頭蛇尾般結束
- 例 After a fast expansion, the company soon fizzled out.
- 中 在迅速擴展營運後，這間公司不久後就結束了。

Smooth over

- 釋 緩和；平息
- 例 Two students had an argument and teacher came to smooth things over between them.
- 中 老師來平息兩位學生之間的爭吵。

Intuition

- 釋 直覺
- 例 Ben can't explain why but his intuition told him that something was wrong.
- 中 Ben無法解釋為什麼，但他的直覺告訴他事情不對。

Show off

釋 炫耀

例 He has just bought a house in central London and is keen to show off his new home.

中 他剛剛在倫敦市中心買了一棟房子,並渴望向人炫耀他的新家。

 **延伸話題**

Councilwoman

A councilwoman is a woman who is a member of local government and is elected by public.

女議員

Councilwoman為人民所選出的政府單位女性成員。

Translator

A translator is a person whose job is to translate one language into a different language.

翻譯家

Translator的工作為將一種語言翻譯成另一種語言。

作者給力回答　　MP3-40

- copious 豐富度　★★★★★★★★★☆
- creative 創意度　★★★★★★☆☆☆
- impressive 深刻度　★★★★★★★★☆☆
- vivid 生動程度　★★★★★★★★☆
- pertinent 切題度　★★★★★★☆☆☆

A second language you want to learn (except English)

A second language I want to learn is Japanese because there are some similarities between Japanese and Mandarin Chinese. Firstly, Japanese has borrowed a lot of Chinese characters. Japanese called it "Kanji". If you can read Chinese, you can easily read Kanji. However, Kanji isn't pronounced the same as Chinese Mandarin. You have to learn how to pronounce each character. Secondly, Japan is very close to my country and they do a lot of business with us. It is always helpful to know

想學的第二外語（除了英語）

我想學的第二外語為日文，因為中文與日文間有許多的共同點。首先，日文從中文引進了許多字彙。日本人將它稱為"漢字"。假如你能讀中文字，你也能輕易地讀漢字。然而，漢字的讀法不同於中文的讀法，你必須學習漢字的發音。第二，日本距離我的國家非常的近，而且與我們做許多的貿易生意。能說一些日文，對與日本做生意有幫

暖身話題

休閒話題

生活話題

常考話題

生活話題

251

some Japanese when you do international business.

Thirdly, it helps you travel around Japan if you can speak basic Japanese. Being able to reading Kanji is also useful when you travel in Japan because you can read signs and street names and often do not need to ask for directions. However, you still need to learn "hiragana" and "katakana" in order to read Japanese newspapers. Although understanding Kanji is an advantage, I still find Japanese is a difficult language. I have to put a lot of effort into it to master this language. Apart from Japanese pronunciation, Japanese grammar and its rules are complicated.

One of the best ways to learn Japanese is to watch Japanese soap opera with Japanese subtitles. I picked up some useful words while watching soup opera. If you know

助。

第三，假如你能説一些基本的日語，能幫助你到日本旅行。尤其能閱讀漢字，對於在日本旅行很有助益的，因為你能在不用問路的情況下，看懂路示指標及路名。然而，你還是要學習平假名及片假名，才能閱讀日文報紙。雖然能讀漢字是個優勢，我還是覺得日文很困難。我必須要花很多精力，才能精通這個語言。除了日文發音外，日文文法及規則也十分地複雜。

其中一個學日文的好方法是看有日文字幕的日本電視劇。我從看日本電視劇中，學到了許多實用的單字。假如你認識一些

some native speakers, language exchange is also a good method to improve your spoken Japanese.

日本母語人士，語言交換也是一個增進日語口說的好方法。

話題拓展

★ **Second language** 第二外語
★ **Similarity** 相似之處
★ **Characters** 字體
★ **Kanji** 漢字
★ **Subtitles** 字幕
★ **Japanese soap dramas with Japanese subtitles** 有日文字幕的日本電視劇
★ **Useful words** 有用的字

「生活話題」

Melissa & Joey — Describe a piece of good news

🌲 影集內容敘述

　　Melissa發現自己懷孕了，當她正打算告訴Joey這個好消息時，Joey卻因忙著準備與銀行的報告，而忙得不可開交。Melissa決定等Joey忙完他的報告後，再跟他提起這個好消息。Joey意外地在垃圾桶看到呈陽性的驗孕棒，並詢問Melissa的姪女Lennox是誰使用過的驗孕棒。Lennox因答應幫Melissa保守秘密，而謊稱是她懷孕了。Joey對於Lennox懷孕之事，十分地緊張，且大張旗鼓幫還是青少年的Lennox準備一些懷孕時期的用品。隔日，Melissa赴醫院再次檢查懷孕結果，但醫生卻表示Melissa並沒有懷孕。因Melissa使用過期的驗孕棒，而懷孕結果並不準確。Melissa回到家中，發現這場誤會時，跟Joey解釋原由。但Joey表示，若Melissa真的懷孕，應該第一時間告訴他，他並不會因忙碌，而忽視了這個大好消息。

影集語彙

In summary
釋 總結來説

例 In summary, this type of new cars can help to reduce pollution.

中 總結來説，這款新車有助於降低環境汙染。

Prep
釋 預習；作好準備；〔英式用法〕學校的功課

例 She is prepping for an interview.

中 她正在準備面試。

Stress out
釋 使某人緊張

例 Examines always stress him out.

中 考試總是令他很緊張。

Relief
釋 解脱；痛苦，負擔的緩和

例 It was a relief to hear that Mary arrived home safe and sound.

中 聽到Mary平安到家的消息，我的負擔完全解脱。

Unbeatable
釋 不能超越的；打不垮的

例 This supermarket is unbeatable because they have high

quality food and reasonable prices.

中 這間超市是打不垮的，因為它的食物品質高，且價格合理。

 延伸話題

Tall order

A tall order is something difficult to achieve or an unreasonable demand. For examples, finishing an urgent project in time is a tall order.

困難的任務

Tall order是指某件難以達成或不合理的要求。舉例來說，完成一件緊急的案子是一個困難的任務。

Study group

A study group is a small group of people who meet to study or discuss a particular subject regularly. It is very popular in high schools, universities or companies.

讀書會

讀書會為定期會面來討論及學習特定科目的小型組織。它目前在高中、大學、及公司皆十分地盛行。

作者給力回答　MP3-41

- copious 豐富度　★★★★★★★★★☆
- creative 創意度　★★★★★★★☆☆☆
- impressive 深刻度　★★★★★★★★☆☆
- vivid 生動程度　★★★★★★★★★☆
- pertinent 切題度　★★★★★★☆☆☆

Describe a piece of good news

I would like to talk about a trip I won in a prize drawing event. When I was a teenager, I liked drink fruit juice. I usually purchase two bottles of fruit juice from convenience stores every day. Since the fruit juice market was very competitive at that time, many fruit juice companies ran marketing campaigns in order to attract new customers. I thought most brands tasted the same, so I usually chose the ones with promotional offers.

描述一則好消息

我想要談我從抽獎活動贏得的旅行。當我還是青少年時，我很喜歡喝果汁。我通常一天會從便利商店買兩瓶的果汁。當時果汁的市場十分的競爭，許多果汁公司發起了許多廣宣活動，以吸引新客群。對我來說，大部分的果汁味道皆相同，我通常會買有促銷活動的品牌。

暖身話題

休閒話題

生活話題

常考話題

生活話題

I noticed that a fruit juice company was having a prize draw event. If you bought two bottles of fruit juice and sent back the fruit juice trademark labels with your contact information, you would have the chance to win a trip to Tokyo. I started collecting their labels after I saw this promotion and sent many labels to the company in the hope of winning.

Three months later, I received a letter from the fruit juice company. They informed me that I had won the competition and would send me two flight tickets to Tokyo. I couldn't believe I had won a prize. I felt very lucky. I decided to give the other ticket to my mother since she had always wanted to go to Tokyo. We went to Tokyo together during my summer holiday and enjoyed our trip very much. I think this marketing campaign was very successful as it offered the incentive consumers wanted.

我當時注意到有一家果汁公司在做抽獎活動。若你買兩瓶果汁，並寄回果汁商標與你的聯絡資料，就有機會贏得東京旅行。我立即開始收集果汁商標，並寄回許多的商標到那間公司。

大約三個月後，我收到一封從果汁公司寄來的信。他們通知我抽中了獎項，並會再寄給我兩張飛東京的機票。我當時不敢相信我贏得了旅行，並且覺得我很幸運。因為我的媽媽一直想到東京旅遊，我決定將另一張機票送給她。我們於暑假期間一同赴東京旅遊，並有著一次愉快的假期。我覺得這個行銷活動很成功，因為它提供了消費者真正想要的激勵獎品。

💬 話題拓展

★ **Marketing campaign** 行銷活動
★ **Fruit juice market** 水果汁市場
★ **Promotion** 促銷
★ **Incentive** 激勵
★ **Competition** 抽獎活動
★ **Two flight tickets to Tokyo** 兩張飛東京的機票
★ **Brand** 品牌

Notes

Where the heart is — Describe an important thing for you

影集內容敘述

　　Gaynor發起了一個清理汙染河川的保育活動，並邀請了護士Zoe共同前往。自願者們積極地撿拾河川中的可利用資源回收物。Gaynor突然看到置於河川中間的一個銀製盒子，奮不顧身的想要取得此盒子。然而，她卻不小心滑落，並傷及手臂。Zoe趕緊幫忙包紮傷口，並告誡她須好好休息，近期不能再從事此類活動。然而，Gaynor瘋狂地想要取回這個盒子，甚至偷取回收品儲藏室的鑰匙，以找回這個盒子。Zoe發現後，與她爭論，Gaynor卻在爭論過程中，身體不適而被送進醫院。Zoe幫她取回銀盒子，並詢問為何此盒子對她這麼重要。原來此盒子是Gaynor的母親年輕時所遺棄的，她的母親當時因隱疾不想連累Gaynor的父親，而假裝對他無感情，逼使他離家出走。當她丈夫離開後，她將對他寄託思念的物品放置在於此盒裡，並丟入河裡。Gaynor當時目擊所有經過，並期盼將來能撿回此盒子。

影集語彙

Kill two birds with one stone

釋　一石二鳥

例　I killed two birds with one stone and visited my friend during a business trip's weekend.

中　我在出差的途中，順便利用週末拜訪我的朋友。一石二鳥。

Out of one's depth

釋　不能勝任；非...所能理解

例　It was out of my depth in the math class, so I hired a math tutor to teach me.

中　由於數學課對我來說太難，我請了一位數學家教來教我。

Vicious circle

釋　惡性循環

例　Many people get caught in a vicious circle of using credit cards to pay off their debts.

中　許多人陷入了用信用卡還債的惡性循環。

At stake

釋　處於危急關頭；冒風險

例　About a hundred jobs will be at stake if our company loses this contract.

中　假如公司失去了這個合約，約一百人的工作會有危險。

Debris

釋 破瓦殘礫

例 The river is littered with debris.

中 河床上到處是破瓦殘礫。

 延伸話題

Conservation

Conservation is a preservation of natural resources, animals or historical and cultural sites.

保育

Conservation為對自然資源、動物、歷史及文化建築的保護行動。

Canal

A canal is an artificial waterway connecting two areas of water, such as lakes, rivers, oceans and so on. It can be used for shipping, travel and irrigation.

運河

Canal為人造的水路,用來連結兩個地區的湖泊、河流、或海洋等。它可用來做運輸、旅行、及灌溉等功用。

作者給力回答　MP3-42

- copious 豐富度　★★★★★★★★★☆
- creative 創意度　★★★★★★★☆☆☆
- impressive 深刻度　★★★★★★★★☆☆
- vivid 生動程度　★★★★★★★★★☆
- pertinent 切題度　★★★★★★★☆☆☆

Describe an important thing for you

My tablet computer is important to me because it helps me to surf the Internet, get information I need and store all my important documents and photos. When I wake up in the morning, I use my tablet computer to check traffic and weather. Unlike traditional laptops or desktop computers, you can turn it on in seconds. You won't waste much time turning it on. Additionally, it's light and compact, so it is convenient to use on a sofa or bed.

描述一件對你重要的事

我的平板電腦對我非常的重要，因為它可讓我上網取得我所需要的資訊，以及存取重要的文件、照片等。每天清晨起床時，我通常會用平板電腦來查交通及天氣。不同於傳統的筆記型電腦或個人電腦，平板電腦只要數秒鐘即可開機。你不用花太多時間在開啟電腦上。此外，它十分地輕巧，你可以輕鬆地在沙發或床上使用。

暖身話題

休閒話題

生活話題

常考話題

生活話題

265

I also use it to check my e-mails, update my status on social media, listen to music, play games, and watch films. My tablet PC comes with a keyboard and a mouse, so I can make it became a laptop if I feel like typing. When I take the train, my tablet computer can also be used as an e-book reader.

Since I use my tablet computer a lot, I usually purchase one with a long battery life, so I can carry it around and not worry about charging it. I realise that a tablet computer is important for me and I can't live without it now. Unfortunately, it is not good for my eyes if I use it for a long time. I have tried to cut down on using the tablet PC but failed. It is force of habit that I use my tablet PC every morning. Technology has changed our lifestyles significantly, and we should look for healthy ways to spend our free time, without being addicted to electronic devices.

我也使用平板電腦來查閱電子郵件、更新我在Facebook上的狀態、聽音樂、玩遊戲、及觀看電影。我的平板電腦附有鍵盤及滑鼠，當我想打字時，它也可以變為筆記型電腦。當我在火車上時，也可以把它用作電子書。

由於我很常使用平板電腦，我通常會買電池壽命較長的產品。這樣我就能帶著它到處走，也不用擔心充電的問題。我了解平板電腦對我的重要性，我的生活也不能沒有它。然而，長期使用對眼睛不好。我試著減少使用平板電腦的時間，但是失敗了。出於習慣，我每天早上都會使用平板電腦。科技改變了我們的生活方式，而我們應該於空閒時間多做些健康有益的事，而不是整天沈迷於電子產品。

話題拓展

★ **Tablet PC** 平板電腦
★ **Laptops** 筆記型電腦
★ **Compact** 小巧的
★ **E-book** 電子書
★ **Battery life** 電池壽命
★ **Our lifestyles** 生活方式
★ **Electronic devices** 電子產品

Notes

Rules of Engagement — Describe a show you have watched

🌿 影集內容敘述

　　Jeff買了一張音樂劇的門票給Audrey做為她的生日禮物。Audrey雖然開心，但希望Jeff能陪她一起去看音樂劇。但Jeff以對音樂劇不感興趣為由而拒絕。趁著Audrey去看音樂劇的空檔，Jeff獨自去參加遊艇展覽。在展覽上，他遇見了一位舊識，這名朋友與Jeff夫婦同樣結婚十二年，但最近分手了，原因是夫妻倆的興趣不合，常各自做自己喜歡的事，久而久之就分道揚鑣。有著朋友的前車之鑑，Jeff開始提高警覺。他跑到戲院門口等待看完音樂劇的老婆，並約她一起共進晚餐。

影集語彙

Drift apart

釋 人與人的關係漸漸疏遠

例 After I moved abroad, my friends and I have drifted apart.

中 在我搬到國外後，我和朋友們的關係漸漸疏遠。

From now on

釋 從現在開始

例 From now on this shop will open until eleven o'clock.

中 從現在開始，這間商店會營業到晚上十一點。

Make fun of

釋 取笑

例 The other children were making fun of her because of her weird outfit .

中 其他的孩子們在取笑她怪異的服裝。

Punctuality

釋 守時

例 Punctuality is very important in Amy's company.

中 守時在Amy的公司是非常重要的。

Unmanly

釋 無男子漢氣概的

例 Ben thinks it is unmanly to watch soppy film.

暖身話題

休閒話題

生活話題

常考話題

生活話題

中 Ben認為看多情傷感的電影是很沒有男子漢氣概的。

延伸話題

Musical

A musical is a play that actors and actresses act, sing and dance during the show.

音樂劇

音樂劇為演員們在舞台上演戲、唱歌、及跳舞的一種表演型式。

Theatre district

A theatre district is an area where most Broadway theatres are located. Both New York Manhattan's theatre district and London West End theatres are considered to be the most successful commercial theatres in the English speaking countries.

劇院區

Theatre district是指百老匯劇院所聚集的地方。紐約曼哈頓及倫敦西區劇院被視為英語國家中最成功的商業劇院。

作者給力回答　MP3-43

- copious 豐富度　★★★★★★★★★☆
- creative 創意度　★★★★★★★☆☆☆
- impressive 深刻度　★★★★★★★★☆☆
- vivid 生動程度　★★★★★★★★★☆
- pertinent 切題度　★★★★★★★☆☆☆

Describe a show you have watched

I would like to talk about a musical I watched in London's West End. The West End of London is well-known for outstanding musicals, which attract thousands of visitors from around the world every year. You can see high quality theatrical performances with well-known actors and actresses performing.

The play I saw was about a fifteen-year-old boy who had autism. He discovered the dead body of a neighbour's dog and wanted to find

描述你曾看過的秀

我想要談我在倫敦看過的一齣音樂劇。倫敦西區因出色的音樂劇表演而知名，它每年吸引成千上萬的國際旅客到訪。你甚至能觀賞到由當紅藝人親自表演的舞台劇。能看到名人的精湛的舞臺演出是一種絕佳的體驗。

我觀賞的音樂劇為描述一名患有高功能自閉症的十五歲少年。當他發現了鄰居家的狗屍體時，便

out who was the dog's murderer. He finally discovered his father's lies during his investigation. This play was a stage adaptation of a best-selling novel in the UK. The show lasted for about three hours and there was an interval during the show. Audiences can get a drink or snacks during the break.

I liked this show because of the acting and teamwork from the actors and actresses. Apart from the actors and actresses' great performances, this show had fantastic scenery and lighting designs. Since the main character traveled to many different places in the show, they used special lighting to indicate different locations he went to. Audiences could easily see if the actors and actresses had moved to a different place. I enjoyed watching this show and would recommend it to my friends if they want to experience London's theatrical world.

決定要追查出兇手來。在偵查過程中,他發現了父親一連串的謊言。這齣劇由一本英國暢銷小說所改編的。整齣劇歷時約三個小時。中場有休息時間,觀眾們可藉中場休息購買飲料及點心。

我喜歡這齣劇的原因為演員們的演技及團隊合作能力。除了演員們精采的演出外,它還有絕佳的舞台及燈光設計。由於主角在劇中到處旅行,他們用特殊的燈光效果來指示出不同的場景。觀眾們即能輕易地了解演員們移動到不同的地點。我很享受觀看此劇,並也會推薦給想要體驗倫敦劇院世界的朋友們。

💬 話題拓展

★ **West End of London** 倫敦西區
★ **Autism** 自閉症
★ **Adaptation** 改編
★ **Interval** 戲劇的幕間休息
★ **Fantastic scene** 佳的舞台
★ **Lighting designs** 燈光設計
★ **Acting and teamwork** 演技和團隊合作

Notes

主題 44

Baby Daddy — Sports

🌲 影集內容敘述

　　Ben和朋友們組了一支壘球隊，並在家樓下的壘球場練球。Ben趁著球賽空檔上樓照顧女兒，並請Riley代勞將設備拿到樓下的練習場。當Ben回到球場時，Riley因她過人的表現，被其他的隊友選為壘球隊隊長。Riley在擔任隊長期間非常好勝，隊員對於Riley過於嚴格的訓練方法實在吃不消，並希望Ben與她溝通，使她辭去隊長的職務。當Riley發現自己過於認真的態度不被其他隊友所接受，難過的在樓頂獨自練球消氣，Ben上樓陪伴她，並聽她訴苦。

影集語彙

Trophy

釋 獎品；獎盃；勝利紀念品

例 This is the first trophy he won from the Olympic games.

中 這是他從奧運所奪下的第一個獎盃。

Workout

釋 鍛鍊，訓練

例 Justin does a thirty minutes workout in the gym everyday.

中 Justin每天在健身房鍛鍊三十分鐘。

Pinch hitter

釋 替補者；代打者

例 He was a pinch hitter for last night's baseball game and performed very well.

中 他是昨天球賽的替補者，且表現十分地出色。

Field

釋 運動場

例 John and his teammates are playing football in a football field.

中 John和他的隊友們正在足球場上踢球。

Goofy

釋 愚笨的；傻的

> 例 Linda is a nice girl, but she is a little goofy.
> 中 Linda是一個好女孩，但有點傻乎乎。

🎈 延伸話題

Home run

In baseball, home run is hitting a ball so far and allows a batter to run around four bases and get a point.

全壘打

在棒球中，全壘打為打擊手打了一支安打，並可跑完四個壘包，並回到本壘得分。

Umpire

Umpire is a person who watches a sport match closely in order to make sure that players obey the rules and the match is played fairly.

裁判

裁判的工作為關注整場球賽，維持比賽公平性，以及確保球員們皆遵守比賽規則。

作者給力回答　MP3-44

- **copious 豐富度** ★★★★★★★★★☆
- **creative 創意度** ★★★★★★★☆☆☆
- **impressive 深刻度** ★★★★★★★★☆☆
- **vivid 生動程度** ★★★★★★★★★☆
- **pertinent 切題度** ★★★★★★★☆☆☆

Describe sports in your country

I would like to talk about baseball and basketball. Baseball is a very popular sport in my country. Young people usually watch baseball games in stadiums or on TV during the weekends. Baseball has been running for over a hundred years in my country. Some baseball teams have performed exceptionally well in many international competitions. However, the development of baseball in my country did not always go smoothly, due to a lack of management.

描述你國家裡的運動

我想要談棒球及籃球。棒球在我的國家是非常受歡迎的一項運動。年青人喜歡於週末時到球場看賽，或看電視轉播。棒球在我國已發展超過一百年的歷史。過去一些棒球隊在國際比賽中也表現的十分出色。然而，由於缺乏管理，我國的棒球發展不總是這麼的順遂。

暖身話題

休閒話題

生活話題

常考話題

生活話題

Since the establishment of the professional baseball league, the number of people who watch baseball games has grown. The professional teams are usually sponsored by leading businesses and named after these businesses. Successful baseball players are regarded as celebrities and earn high salaries. Therefore, more and more young people want to become baseball players. Our government is also promoting baseball and building stadiums for games.

Another popular sport in my country is basketball. Since there is not much room to build stadiums in my country, playing basketball is easier. You can see basketball courts everywhere in my country. Young people usually play basketball in courts after school or work. I think basketball is a great sport for teenagers because it can help them become taller and learn teamwork skills.

自從職棒成立後，觀看棒球的人數與日俱增。職棒球隊通常為大企業贊助成立，並以其企業名稱為名。成功的棒球選手在社會上被視為名人，並賺得不錯的待遇。因此，愈來愈多的年輕人想要成為棒球選手。我們的政府也積極推廣棒球，並興建棒球場。

另一個熱門的運動為籃球。由於我國的可用空間不多，打籃球為一項較方便的運動。我國的籃球場隨處可見。年輕人通常於下課或下班後，在籃球場上打球。籃球為適合青少年的運動，因為它可幫助青少年們增高，且訓練團隊能力。

💬 話題拓展

★ **Stadiums** 球場
★ **International competitions** 國際比賽
★ **Smoothly** 順利地
★ **Professional baseball league** 職棒
★ **Teamwork** 團隊合作
★ **Basketball** 籃球
★ **Teenagers** 青少年

Notes

_____

_____

_____

_____

_____

_____

90210 — Describe an outdoor activity

🌿 影集內容敘述

　　Naomi和Liam開始交往後，Naomi一直很認真的看待這待感情，不段地想討好Liam，但她總覺得彼此間沒有火花。當Naomi看到Ives與 Liam如膠似漆的友情後，決定向Ives求助，希望她能藉由對Liam的了解，來給她一些建議。Ives起初不想介入此事，但禁不起Naomi的苦苦哀求，同意與他們一起出遊，來找出他們之間的問題。由於Liam喜歡戶外活動，三人一同於週末登山健行。不擅戶外運動的Naomi，在爬山時氣喘呼吁，但為了討Liam的歡心，她只好豁出去了。Ives在登山過程中，一直找機會消遣Naomi，Naomi這時才頓悟Ives其實心中一直暗戀著Liam。兩個女人之間的戰火也在此時愈燒愈旺。在一次的衝浪活動中，Naomi因不滿Ives故意碰撞她，倆人便大打出手。在Liam趕來勸架後，Naomi坦承她受夠了掩飾真實的自己來討好他，並決定要做回自己。Liam也表示他其實是喜歡真正的Naomi，而不是裝模作樣的她。

🚗 影集語彙

Rub off on
釋 因相處而產生影響
例 I hope that my bad temper wouldn't rub off on my children.
中 我希望我的壞脾氣不要對我的孩子產生影響。

Slack off
釋 鬆懈
例 Don't slack off. You need to pass the exam and go to the top university.
中 別鬆懈了。你要通過測試，並考到最高學府。

Come clean
釋 全盤招供
例 David came clean and confessed what he has been doing.
中 David 全盤招供他所作的一切。

Opinionated
釋 固執己見的
例 She is an opinionated woman who always thinks she is right.
中 她是一個固執的女人，她總是認為她是對的。

Underestimate
釋 低估；看輕

> **例** Don't underestimate Susan. Although she is tiny, she is good at physical exercise.
>
> **中** 別低估了Susan。她雖然嬌小，但很擅長體育活動。

延伸話題

Surfing

Surfing is an outdoor activity of riding on a wave on a special board, which carries surfers toward the shore.

衝浪運動

衝浪為一種乘坐在衝浪板上駕浪，藉由海浪力量，將衝浪者帶回岸邊的戶外活動。

Hiking

Hiking is a long walk in the mountains or countryside. Hiking is usually for recreational purposes.

健行

健行為在山區或郊區的長途徒步旅行。健行通常視為一種消遣活動。

作者給力回答　💿 MP3-45

- **copious** 豐富度　★★★★★★★★★☆
- **creative** 創意度　★★★★★★☆☆☆
- **impressive** 深刻度　★★★★★★★★☆
- **vivid** 生動程度　★★★★★★★★☆
- **pertinent** 切題度　★★★★★★☆☆☆

Describe an outdoor activity

　　An outdoor activity I enjoy doing in my leisure time is hiking. I went to the Snowdonia National Park in north Wales with my friends a few years ago. Snowdonia is a popular tourist destination in the UK, especially for hiking and sightseeing. We stayed in a village next to a mountain in the Snowdonia National　Park. It has the most beautiful natural scenery I have ever seen. Snow-capped mountains surrounded the village. There were waterfalls, rivers, lakes, hills, and green fields around the village.

戶外活動

　　我於空閒時間喜歡做的戶外活動為健行。幾年前，我與朋友們一同到北威爾斯的Snowdonia國家公園旅行。Snowdonia為英國的一處熱門的景點，尤其是健行及遊覽最為知名。我們住在Snowdonia國家公園旁的一座村莊。這個村莊裡有著我見過最美麗的自然景色，白雪覆蓋山頭的群山圍繞著村莊。村莊裡並有著瀑布，河流、湖區、山丘、綠地等自然景觀。

暖身話題

休閒話題

生活話題

常考話題

生活話題

283

We arrived in Snowdonia in the evening and stayed in a hotel at the bottom of the mountain. We left for the summit next morning. It was not easy to reach the mountaintop because there were many steep hills and roads in the mountain. We were exhausted when we reached the mountaintop. However, the view from the top of mountain was breathtaking. If you don't want to hike, you can also take a train to the summit of Mount Snowdon.

Apart from hiking, you can also do boat trips, water sports, go fishing and cycling. I would recommend this activity to friends who enjoy seeing natural scenery. You can take the opportunity to admire the views of the countryside and exercise at the same time. This is a great way to escape from hectic city life.

我們於晚間抵達 Snowdonia，並下榻於山腳下的一間飯店。隔日清晨出發前往山頂。登山的過程並不順遂，因為山中有許多陡峭的山丘及道路。當我們抵達頂峰時，已精疲力盡。然而，從山頂望去有著令人驚嘆的美景。若你不爬山，也可乘坐山頂火車到山峰。

除了登山，也有搭船、玩水上運動、釣魚、騎自行車等活動。我會向喜愛自然景色的朋友推薦這項活動。不但可欣賞郊外景色，也可以健身。這是一個遠離繁忙都市生活的好去處。

話題拓展

★ **Snowdonia National Park in north Wales** 北威爾斯的Snowdonia 國家公園旅行
★ **A popular tourist destination** 熱門的觀光景點
★ **Sightseeing** 觀光
★ **Mountaintop** 山頂
★ **Breathtaking** 令人驚嘆的
★ **Natural scenery** 自然景色
★ **Water sports** 水上運動
★ **Go fishing** 釣魚
★ **Cycling** 騎自行車

Notes

暖身話題

休閒話題

生活話題

常考話題

生活話題

Rules of Engagement — Describe a foreign celebrity

🌿 影集內容敘述

　　Audrey抱怨Jeff經常忘東忘西的，無法幫忙處理家中的事務。Jeff為了讓老婆消氣，承諾會幫忙於一個月前預約法國餐廳的位子。然而，當他正打電話預約時，一個朋友的簡訊讓他忘了這檔事。一個月後，他突然想起此事，趕緊打電話預約位子。然而，這間餐廳十分的受歡迎，所有的用餐時段皆訂滿了。Jeff想起他的朋友Adam曾說過有些餐廳會保留座位給名人，便興起假扮名人的念頭。他先向Audrey提議用餐當天彼此互相扮演成名人的遊戲，Audrey以為這只是個遊戲，並不知道他打的主意，就答應佯裝為妮可基嫚。當兩人赴餐廳時，他先支開Audrey，並向服務生謊稱他與妮可基嫚一同前來，並順利的取得兩個用餐時段的座位。然而，當倆人入座時，謊言還是被拆穿了，倆人因此尷尬的離開。

🚗 **影集語彙**

Count on
🔸 依賴；信賴；指望
🔸 Children always count on their parents to help them.
🔸 小孩們總是期待父母來幫助他們。

Common ground
🔸 共同點
🔸 Although they are from different backgrounds, they still found common ground.
🔸 雖然他們來自不同的背景，他們還是發現了共同點。

Sceptical
🔸 懷疑的
🔸 Many people remain sceptical about the new research.
🔸 大部分的人對這項研究持懷疑的態度。

On the fence
🔸 猶豫不決
🔸 Rita is on the fence about quitting her job and going back to university.
🔸 Rita正猶豫不決是否該辭掉工作，並回大學唸書。

Blow it
🔸 錯失機會

> 例 It was a great opportunity for her to get that job but she blew it by saying the wrong things.
>
> 中 這是幫助她找到工作的好機會，但她因說錯話而錯失機會。

 延伸話題

The last minute

The last minute means the last possible time or opportunity to do something. Some people wait until the last minute before the event, such as booking a hotel or preparing exams.

最後一刻

The last minute是形容在最後一刻或把握機會去做某事。有些人會在事情發生前的最後一刻才開始行動，像是訂旅館、或準備考試。

Celebrity

A celebrity is a famous person who is easily recognised by the general public, especially in entertainment or sport. They are the centre of attention everywhere they go.

名人

Celebrity指易被民眾認出的知名人士。他們通常為眾人矚目的焦點。

 作者給力回答　MP3-46

- copious 豐富度　★★★★★★★★★☆
- creative 創意度　★★★★★★☆☆☆
- impressive 深刻度　★★★★★★★★☆☆
- vivid 生動程度　★★★★★★★★★☆
- pertinent 切題度　★★★★★★☆☆☆

Describe a foreign celebrity

When I was a student, I worked as a waitress in a five-star hotel during the summer break. The advantage of working in a hotel is to see many different people, including celebrities. Oncc, I saw a famous actor from Hong Kong in front of the hotel restaurant . He was my favourite actor when I was a teenager. I was shocked and couldn't believe my eyes. I stared at him in amazement and couldn't say a word.

He noticed that I was looking at

描述一位國外名人

當我還是學生時，我於暑假期間在一間五星級的飯店擔任餐廳服務生。在飯店工作的好處為有機會能見識到形形色色的人，像是名人。我記得我在飯店的餐廳前，見過一位知名的香港演員。他是我青少年時期最喜愛的演員。我當時十分地驚訝，不敢相信這是事實，並且驚奇地望著他，一句話也說不出來。

他注意到我在看著

暖身話題

休閒話題

生活話題

常考話題

生活話題

him, so he came to say hello to me. I was so happy and nervous. He told me that he was here to shoot a film. I told him that I really like watching his films and asked him if I could have his autograph. He left after giving me his autograph. It was a great experience and something I can share with my friends.

I also saw other celebrities when I worked there. They came to the hotel for different purposes. Some of them stayed in the hotel during film shoots. Some of them met friends in hotel restaurants or came to the hotel for public events. They always looked nice and well-dressed. I feel sorry for them because celebrities don't really have privacy and have to care about what they look like all the time.

他，便走過來跟我打招呼。我當時既開心又緊張。他告訴我他來這裡拍攝電影。我說我很喜歡看他的電影，可否向他要簽名。他在給我親筆簽名後離開。這是一次很棒的經驗，並且也是我可以跟朋友分享的話題。

在那間飯店工作的期間，我見過許多的名人。他們基於不同的目的到飯店來。有些名人在拍攝電影期間住宿飯店，有些名人到飯店餐廳見朋友，有些則來參加宴會。他們總是保持最佳狀態，並穿得很體面。我其實為他們感到抱歉，因為這些名人缺乏隱私空間，並且隨時要注意他們的儀態。

話題拓展

★ **A five-star hotel** 五星級的飯店
★ **Amazement** 驚奇
★ **Film shooting** 電影拍攝
★ **Autograph** 親筆簽名
★ **Public events** 公眾活動
★ **Well-dressed** 穿得很體面的
★ **Privacy** 隱私

Notes

Melissa & Joey — Describe a task you did with others

🍃 影集內容敘述

　　Melissa正開心地籌備著婚禮，婆婆卻突然造訪，並打算全權統籌婚禮。然而，Melissa和婆婆在婚禮佈置上的意見不合。Melissa不想因此得罪了婆婆，但也不想讓婆婆插手處理婚禮佈置。她請先生Joey幫忙出主意，Joey想到一個兩全其美的辦法。Melissa之前挑了五間婚禮攝影，每間都很喜歡，遲遲無法做決定。若讓婆婆全權處理婚禮攝影，不論她選哪一間，Melissa皆不會介意。另一方面，婆婆忙著接洽婚禮攝影事宜，也沒空干涉婚禮佈置。然而，婆婆卻在意料之外請了一位Joey不想邀請的人來擔任婚禮攝影。

🚗 影集語彙

Unannounced

釋 未通知的；突然的

例 Her mother-in-law arrived unannounced and took control of the wedding.

中 她的婆婆突然出現，並控制了婚禮。

Lift a finger

釋 幫一點忙；盡舉手之勞

例 Sean have never lifted a finger to help with cleaning.

中 Sean從來不主動幫忙打掃。

Come around

釋 改變主意；讓步

例 She came around to my point of view after I persuaded her.

中 在我的說服下，她終於改變主意了。

Take the plunge

釋 經過一番考量後打定主意

例 After living together for ten years, they are finally taking the plunge .

中 在同居十年後，他們終於打定主意要結婚了。

Misleading

釋 使人誤解的；誤導的

> **例** This advertisement contains misleading information.
> **中** 這個廣告含有令人誤解的訊息。

🎈延伸話題

Task

A task is a piece of work that needs to be done within a period of time.

任務

任務為在既定的時限內，需完成的工作。

Doily

Doily is a small piece of paper with a lace pattern. It is used as a decoration on a plate before putting a cake on it.

圓形墊子

Doily為一塊小型含花邊的紙。它是放在盤子上墊在蛋糕底下裝飾用。

作者給力回答　　MP3-47

- copious 豐富度　★★★★★★★★★☆
- creative 創意度　★★★★★☆☆☆
- impressive 深刻度　★★★★★★★☆☆
- vivid 生動程度　★★★★★★★★☆
- pertinent 切題度　★★★★★★☆☆☆

Describe a task you did with others

I have worked on several projects with my classmates and colleagues in my life. I would like to talk about a project I worked on with my classmates when I was at college. It was a business project in the last year of university and I had to work with four team members.

We needed to conduct an interview with a business and work on a report based on information we collected. We chose a leading retailer in the capital city. I planned a list of

描述一件與他人合作的專案

我曾經與同學及同事合作過許多專案。我想要談一件在大學時期與同學共同合作的專案。這是在入學最後一年的一個商業專案，當時需與四個團員合作。

我們需要與一間企業進行訪談，並將訪談的資料彙集成報告。我們選了一間在首都的頂尖零售企業。我列出了一連串的任

暖身話題

休閒話題

生活話題

常考話題

生活話題

tasks and assigned them to our team members. My job was to contact this business and arrange a face to face interview.

After we set a date for the interview, I made a list of interview questions and discussed it with my team members. The interview went very well and we collected the information we needed for our project. After the interview, we started drafting the report. We held a meeting to discuss the preliminary report and made a few modifications. After a few meetings, we finalised our report and submitted it. It was a great experience because I learnt how to work in a team, control the project status and liaise with a business. In addition, I realised that good communication is very important because you need to make sure that all the team members are on the same page.

務，並將它們分配給團員們。我的工作為與該企業聯繫，並安排訪談。

在我們設定訪談日期後，我製定訪談問題表並與團員討論。訪談進行的很順利，並且收集到專案所需的資料。在訪談後，我們開始草擬報告內容。我們召集了一個會議討論初步報告，並進行修改。在經歷了幾次會議後，最後完成了報告並提交。這是一次很寶貴的經驗，因為我學到了團隊合作，掌控專案進度，及與企業聯繫。另外，我也認知到好的溝通技巧十分地重要，因為你要確保團員們的意見一致。

話題拓展

★ **Team members** 團員
★ **A preliminary report** 初步報告
★ **Modifications** 修改
★ **Communication** 溝通
★ **On the same page** 意見一致
★ **Control the project status** 掌控專案進度
★ **Liaise with a business** 企業聯繫

Notes

90210 — Describe a newspaper you read before

🌲 影集內容敘述

　　Mr. Cannon成為學校的一名新任指導教師，並將指導學生發行報紙 - The Blaze。在第一次與學生見面的會議上，Naomi和Mr. Cannon因意見不合而發生了一些小爭執。隨後，Mr. Cannon請Naomi單獨到教室裡，要求她道歉。但Naomi拒絕，Mr. Cannon便決定將她踢出The Blaze報紙。Naomi對新聞工作充滿熱忱，並想返回The Blaze報紙。她試著請朋友們支持她，但朋友們皆認為當時是Naomi的言語不當所造成的。在孤立無援的情況下，她竟然向朋友撒謊說Mr. Cannon對她言語性騷擾，以便取得朋友們的幫助。她沒想到的是，這個謊言愈演愈烈，到無法輕易收拾的情況。

🚗 影集語彙

Tabloid

釋 小報

例 Richard enjoys reading tabloid newspaper on the way to work.

中 Richard喜歡在通勤時間閱讀小報。

Intern

釋 實習生

例 Annabel worked in a bank as an intern after she graduated from a university.

中 Annabel在大學畢業後，在一間銀行做實習生。

Out of line

釋 行為欠妥

例 He lost his job because he stepped out of line.

中 他因行為欠妥而失去工作。

Bump into

釋 巧遇；和某人不期而遇

例 Vicky bumped into an old classmate on the street.

中 Vicky在街上巧遇舊同學。

Paranoid

釋 多疑的

> 例 She started feeling paranoid about being pickpocketed after she lost her wallet.
>
> 中 她自從錢包被偷後，就開始疑神疑鬼的。

 延伸話題

Extracurricular

An extracurricular activity is not a part of school or college course that students usually take.

課外的

Extracurricular為形容非學校或大學內的課程。

Academia

Academia is an area or community related to education, especially in universities or colleges.

學術界

Academia指與教育有關的領域或群體，特別指在大學或學院。

作者給力回答

- copious 豐富度　★★★★★★★★★☆
- creative 創意度　★★★★★★☆☆☆
- impressive 深刻度　★★★★★★★★☆☆
- vivid 生動程度　★★★★★★★★☆
- pertinent 切題度　★★★★★★☆☆☆

Describe a newspaper

I want to talk about a newspaper I read in the morning. This newspaper is designed for commuters who live around the city. You can get free copies of the newspaper at underground stations. I usually read it on the train when I go to work. This newspaper is packed with comprehensive national and international news, editorials, and useful information. I like this newspaper because it listens to the general public's views. Some newspapers prefer to report on news from a certain political party, they

描述報紙

　　我想要談我每日讀的晨報。這份報紙是專門為市區的通勤族所設計的。你可以在地鐵站取得免費的報紙。我通常於早上通勤上班時，在火車上閱讀。這份報紙充滿著綜合廣泛的國內及國際新聞，社論及實用的資訊。我喜歡這份報紙的原因為它聽得進大眾的聲音。大部分的報紙傾向於某一政黨，他們並沒有公正的評論。

暖身話題

休閒話題

生活話題

常考話題

生活話題

don't have unbiased opinions.

My favourite part of this newspaper is a forum section, which allows the general public to discuss recent news or issues. Readers can send their views and comments to editors via texts or e-mails. I enjoy reading their comments because it helps me to understand the general public's views and opinions.

The other thing I like about this newspaper is that it conducts surveys of public opinion regularly. The survey topics are about issues the general public is interested in, such as some political policy, environmental and transport issues. This newspaper also has a lot of international news articles. It has good examples from other countries, so it helps us to think what we can do to improve our country. They have launched a digital version of this newspapers recently, so I can also read it on my phone or tablet PC.

我最喜歡這份報紙的部分為它的論壇。這個論壇可以讓大眾討論最新的時事及議題。讀者們可以將他們的想法及建議用簡訊或電子郵件的方式寄給編輯。我喜歡讀這些評論的原因是，它可幫助我了解社會大眾的觀點。

另一個喜愛這份報紙的原因為，它定期舉行民意調查。調查的主題為一般大眾所感興趣的議題，像是政策、及環境及交通問題。這份報紙也包含了許多國際新聞。它會借鏡其他國家的優點，如此可幫助人民了解如何改善國家的生活。它近來也發起了電子版本，我可用我的手機或平板電腦閱讀。

💬 話題拓展

- ★ **Morning newspaper** 晨報
- ★ **Commuters** 通勤族
- ★ **General public** 社會大眾
- ★ **Editors** 編輯
- ★ **Forum** 論壇
- ★ **Surveys** 調查
- ★ **Digital version** 電子版本

Notes

Baby Daddy — A person you want to become one day

🌿 影集內容敘述

　　Ben的好友Tucker三年前從法學院輟學後，就去追求他所嚮往的電視台的工作。然而，他的父親觀念保守，一直希望兒子能成為一名律師。不敢告訴父親事實的Tucker，瞞騙父親他從法學院畢業後，成為執業律師。由於父親幾乎不造訪紐約，Tucker以為可以一路瞞騙過關。然而，某日父親突然來電說他在紐約，想要參觀他的律師事務所。Tucker藉由朋友Ben和Riley的幫忙下，再次騙過父親。但在巧遇父親的一名律師朋友後，這名律師朋友邀請Tucker到他的公司上班。Tucker覺得無法再隱瞞下去了，決定向父親坦白。然而，父親在知情後，大發雷霆離去。Ben為了幫助Tucker挽回其父子感情，特地到他父親下榻的飯店，請求他再給Tucker一次解釋的機會。Tucker與父親見面後，說出他所追求的夢想，父親聽完之後，覺得很感動，也為兒子感到驕傲。

影集語彙

Test the water
- 釋 試探某人對某事的意見
- 例 Before you lunch a new product, you should commission market research to test the water and determine consumer response.
- 中 在你推出新產品前,你應該先做市調來試水溫,並測定消費者的回應。

Clumsy
- 釋 笨手笨腳的
- 例 Ian was very clumsy and bumped into a door this morning.
- 中 Ian今天早上笨手笨腳的撞上門。

Hilarious
- 釋 極好笑的;極有趣的
- 例 This is my favourite comedy. It is hilarious.
- 中 這是我最喜愛的喜劇。它超好笑的。

So-called
- 釋 所謂的
- 例 Peter's so-called friend stole his wallet.
- 中 Peter所謂的朋友偷了他的錢包。

In other words

釋 換句話說

例 Johnny said he might not go to the wedding. In other words, he can't make it.

中 Johnny 說他或許不能參加婚禮。換句話說，他不會參加婚禮。

 **延伸話題**

Renaissance

Renaissance is the revival of European art, literature and learning during the 14th, 15th and 16th centuries.

文藝復興

Renaissance指歐洲藝術、文學、學習在14到17世紀的復興時期。

Fair

A fair is a public event where you can buy things, play games and attend competitions to win prizes.

遊樂會

Fair指一種可以購物、玩遊戲、參加競賽活動贏得獎品的遊樂會。

作者給力回答　 MP3-49

- copious 豐富度　★★★★★★★★★☆
- creative 創意度　★★★★★★☆☆☆
- impressive 深刻度　★★★★★★★★☆☆
- vivid 生動程度　★★★★★★★★★☆
- pertinent 切題度　★★★★★★☆☆☆

A person you want to become one day

When I was a teenager, my dream job was to become a successful businesswoman and travel around the world. This is why I chose to study business related subjects at university. I know speaking a second language is helpful for international business, so I worked very hard to improve my language skills.

One of my mother's friends has been my role model since I was young. She is a successful businesswoman and started her

你想成為的人

當我還是青少年時，我夢想成為一位成功的女商人，並且在世界各地到處跑。這也是我為何選讀商學相關科目。我認知到會說第二外語可幫助拓展國際生意，所以我很努力學習語言。

我還小時，我母親的一位朋友是我的仿傚的對象。她是一位成功的女商人，並於二十年前白手起

暖身話題

休閒話題

生活話題

常考話題

生活話題

307

business from scratch about twenty years ago. She had a small factory in the beginning. Her business has expanded over two decades. She owns factories and offices in Asia and now exports electronic products to the United States and Europe. Since her business expanded rapidly, her family members have joined her company to help her. She is always flying to different countries to meet clients and develop business.

She is hard-working and has considerable business acumen. However, she told me she is not perfect. She made some wrong business decisions in the past but she has learnt from her mistakes. I think if you are in a business, you need to take risks and learning from your mistakes. I enjoy talking to her and learn from her experience. I really hope that I can become a successful businesswoman like her one day.

家。公司剛起步時，她擁有著一個小型的工廠。二十年後，她的生意已拓展成一間大型企業。現在她在亞洲擁有數家工廠及辦公室，並將產品銷往歐美地區。由於她的生意迅速擴展開來，她的家人也一同加入幫忙她。她總是在各個國家出差拜訪客戶及擴展生意。

她很勤奮努力也十分地精明。然而，她告訴我她也不是完美的。在她的職業生涯中，也曾做過一些錯誤的決策，但她從中學得教訓。我認為做生意總是難免要冒險，及從錯誤中吸取教訓。我很喜歡跟她聊天，並從她身上學到東西。希望有朝一日我能成為跟她一樣成功的女商人。

💬 話題拓展

★ **Businesswoman** 女商人
★ **Role model** 模範
★ **Language skill** 語言能力
★ **Start from scratch** 從零開始
★ **Wrong business decisions** 錯誤的決策
★ **Lessons** 教訓
★ **Take risks** 冒險

Notes

The Big Bang Theory — Describe an elderly family member

🌱 影集內容敘述

　　Howard希望Bernadette婚後能搬進他家與他的媽媽共同居住，但Bernadette十分地反對這個提議。Howard建議Bernadette於週末到他家過夜，以試著了解是否能與他的媽媽共處。Bernadette起初無法適應Howard媽媽的大嗓門，及不顧他人隱私的習慣。但經過一夜的相處後，她意外地融入了Howard家的習慣。Bernadette除了和他媽媽一同做早餐給Howard，也學起Howard媽媽開始以大嗓門的說話方式與他家人對話。

🚗 影集語彙

Set foot in

釋 到達

例 Andrew does not like watching movies. He refuses to set foot in a cinema.

中 Andrew不喜歡看電影，他拒絕進入電影院。

Give and take

釋 互相忍讓

例 There has to be some give and take in every marriage.

中 每段婚姻總是要互相忍讓。

Make a move

釋 動身

例 Thank you for your hospitality. It is late. We'd better make a move.

中 感謝你的款待。很晚了，我們該走了。

Inevitable

釋 無法避免的

例 Eventually the inevitable happened and Sean had a car accident after a few drinks.

中 最後無法避免的事發生了，Sean在酒後駕車發生了車禍。

暖身話題

休閒話題

生活話題

常考話題

生活話題

Moody

釋 喜怒無常的

例 Maggie is a moody teenager. It is so difficult to predict what she thinks.

中 Maggie為一個喜怒無常的青少年。很難去猜測她在想什麼。

 延伸話題

Yearbook

A yearbook is a book published once a pear and contains information and pictures about what happened in the past one year of school or college. It is commonly used in the United States.

年刊

Yearbook 為一年發行一次的刊物，包含過去一年在學校或大學裡的相片及所發生的事件。年刊在美國廣泛使用。

Trial run

A trial run is a test of a new system, product or method to find out its effectiveness, especially for a new product launch.

試驗

Trial run 為測試一個新系統、產品、或方法，以了解其適用性，尤其是新產品發佈的試驗。

 作者給力回答　MP3-50

- copious 豐富度　★★★★★★★★★☆
- creative 創意度　★★★★★★☆☆☆
- impressive 深刻度　★★★★★★★★☆☆
- vivid 生動程度　★★★★★★★★★☆
- pertinent 切題度　★★★★★★☆☆☆

Describe an elderly family member

I would like to talk about my mother. I spent nearly twenty five years living with her before I pursued a career in the city. She is a caring, warmhearted, and generous person. She has two children and made a lot of sacrifices for her family. My mother cared about our education and health. I still remember when she took us to a bookstore and tried to find suitable textbooks for us.

She is a conservative lady and doesn't really show how much she

描述家裡的長輩

我想要談我的母親。在我到都市求職前，我花了近二十五年的時間與她生活。她是一位關懷人、熱心腸、及慷慨大方的人。她有兩個孩子，也為家庭做出許多犧牲。我母親很重視我們的教育及健康。我還記得她曾帶我們到書店，試著找尋適合我們的教科書。

她是一位保守的女性，不曾表現出她有多麼

暖身話題

休閒話題

生活話題

常考話題

生活話題

loves me. I found she loves me very much when I decided to study abroad for one year. She was so sad and didn't want me to go. I didn't know this decision would upset her so much. However, she finally agreed, realizing that this would be good for my career. I could become independent and learn more skills when studying abroad.

I had many pleasant memories with her. When I was one year old, my mother hosted a birthday party for me. When I was ten years old, she took my brother and I to an amusement park in Hong Kong. She took many photos and kept them in a family photo album, so we can browse these photos when we are older. I enjoy seeing these photos because they bring back pleasant memories of the past. I love her very much and appreciate what she has done for our family.

地愛我們。我發現她愛我至深，是從我決定出國留學一年開始。她當時很傷心，也不想我離開家。我當時並不知道這個決定讓她這麼難過。然而，她最後決定讓我出國留學，因她了解這樣做是對我好，可讓我學習獨立及更多的能力。

我和她有許多美好的回憶。當我一歲時，我的母親幫我辦了一場生日派對。當我十歲時，她帶我和弟弟到香港的遊樂園。她拍了許多照片，並保留在家庭相簿裡。我們可在年長時回顧這些照片。我十分喜愛看這些相片，因它們讓我想起過去那些美好的點滴。我十分地愛她，並感謝她為我們家庭做的貢獻。

💬 話題拓展

★ **Generous** 慷慨的
★ **Sacrifice** 犧牲
★ **Textbook** 教科書
★ **Study abroad** 出國留學
★ **An amusement park** 遊樂園
★ **Photo album** 相簿
★ **Memories** 回憶

Notes

英語學習—生活・文法・考用—

定價：NT$369元/K$115元
規格：320頁/17＊23cm/MP3

定價：NT$380元/HK$119元
規格：320頁/17＊23cm/MP3

定價：NT$349元/HK$109元
規格：352頁/17＊23cm

定價：NT$380元/HK$119元
規格：288頁/17＊23cm/MP3

定價：NT$329元/HK$103元
規格：352頁/17＊23cm

定價：NT$349元/HK$109元
規格：304頁/17＊23cm

定價：NT$380元/HK$119元
規格：352頁/17＊23cm

定價：NT$369元/HK$115元
規格：304頁/17＊23cm/MP3

定價：NT$380元/HK$119元
規格：304頁/17＊23cm/MP3

英語學習－職場系列－

定價：NT$349元/HK$109元
規格：320頁/17＊23cm

定價：NT$360元/HK$113元
規格：328頁/17＊23cm

定價：NT$349元/HK$109元
規格：304頁/17＊23cm

定價：NT$360元/HK$113元
規格：320頁/17＊23cm

定價：NT$369元/HK$115元
規格：312頁/17＊23cm/MP3

定價：NT$369元/HK$115元
規格：320頁/17＊23cm

定價：NT$360元/HK$113元
規格：288頁/17＊23cm/MP3

定價：NT$329元/HK$103元
規格：304頁/17＊23cm

定價：NT$369元/HK$115元
規格：328頁/17＊23cm/MP3

Learn Smart！049

"猴腮雷" 雅思口說 7+ (MP3)

作　　者	詹宜婷
封面構成	高鍾琪
內頁構成	菩薩蠻數位文化有限公司

發 行 人	周瑞德
企劃編輯	陳韋佑
校　　對	陳欣慧、饒美君、魏于婷
印　　製	大亞彩色印刷製版股份有限公司
初　　版	2015 年 8 月
定　　價	新台幣 369 元
出　　版	倍斯特出版事業有限公司
電　　話	(02) 2351-2007
傳　　真	(02) 2351-0887
地　　址	100 台北市中正區福州街 1 號 10 樓之 2
E - m a i l	best.books.service@gmail.com

港澳地區總經銷	泛華發行代理有限公司
地　　　　址	香港新界將軍澳工業邨駿昌街 7 號 2 樓
電　　　　話	(852) 2798-2323
傳　　　　真	(852) 2796-5471

國家圖書館出版品預行編目(CIP)資料

```
猴腮雷" IELTS 口說 7+ / 詹宜婷著. --
初版. -- 臺北市 : 倍斯特, 2015.08
面 ; 公分. -- (Learn smart! ;49)
ISBN 978-986-91915-2-4(平裝附光碟片)
1.國際英語語文測試系統 2.考
試指南
805.189                    104013330
```